DELECTABLE

PHOENIX ASH

B.LOVE PUBLICATIONS PRESENTS

Copyright © 2020 by Phoenix Ash

All rights reserved.

No part of this book may be reproduced in any form or by any electronic or mechanical means, including information storage and retrieval systems, without written permission from the author, except for the use of brief quotations in a book review.

DEDICATION

For us romantics, who yearn for that wondrous love. That pit of the belly tingle that surges through, infecting our blood, electrifying our hearts, adding confidence to our walk. The forever that takes care of us, soothes us, lifts us.

Do yourself a favor and allow yourself to dream. Don't be so easy to believe that what you desire is impossible, unattainable, or non-existent. It's okay to fall into something that takes your breath away.

Sure, it's scary and you worry about it not working out. But as evidence has shown, hearts recover. It's all the goo that's in our minds that slow the mending. Let your soul breathe in all that's good in love. Let it free you.

BITTER TASTE OF *hooch*

AT TEN MINUTES AFTER SEVEN, THE SUN WAS SETTLING ONTO the horizon. Tapping her thumbs against the steering wheel, as the radio thumped a collection of classic dance titles, curated by a local teen DJ, Joi let her car window down and inhaled. The brisk wind pinked her cheeks as it brushed by. Rustling leaves yielded to the pausing traffic. An air of calm washed over the city.

Spring had always represented a sense of renewal in Joi's mind. Something about the scent of blooming flowers, nighttime drizzles, and the buzzing energy of those thankful for the break in weather, gave her hope of change. Since her teenage years, the increase in frowns and murmurs, frost-tipped noses, shivering limbs, along with the lists of complaints that came as a result of the coldness of winter, would cause her to feel unsettled. Sensing Joi's empathetic funk, her mother and sister would soothe her spirit by baking chocolate cake. They'd all sit around the kitchen island contesting each other, shoveling forkfuls into their mouths, until Joi was coughing and spitting crumbs, doubling over with laughter. As if the Universe was familiar with her remedy, her eye caught sight of a baker's café, boasting a pending grand opening on New Castle Avenue.

"Where were you all winter?" Joi shouted, playfully. Still, her heart cheered with the idea of indulging in chocolate more often than the holiday baking her mother had settled into.

As a woman in her thirties, Joi hated that she could still feel the routine uneasiness of the seasons. Lately, it had made itself way too comfortable in her home. *"I don't see why we have to go to the movies. We've got it all right here in the living room. Literally, every streaming service known to man, we have. My hours at the Warehouse are what pays the bills. Laying up with you all day is not exactly a reason to miss payment on my car note,"* Gordon's words echoed through her memory. With the reemergence of the sun, she hoped for repaired love, forehead kisses, and at the very least, Gordon would take a few days off.

Careening her car around the corner, Joi reflected on her day. It had been a long one at the Trailblazer Community College Admissions Office. A glitch in the computer system sent a host of acceptances to students they merely intended to request transcripts from. *It was probably that damn Caprice. The girl's a lingering senior and none of us need to question why, now.*

Routinely, Joi was the recipient as well as the cleanup crew for Caprice's catastrophic errors. It seemed every other week she was handing out misinformation to other students or flipping a switch that would send the bulk of the administrative staff into a frenzy. All in the name of appearing as though she was working. And it never failed. The day after pushing some "do not press" button, she'd call out sick, leaving the rest of the team to sanitize her mess and get their asses chewed out for it.

"Spring Break did not come fast enough. A whole blessing to have a week without tolerating her over-made-up face. I swear her eyebrows look like one of my niece's chalk drawings. I'll be the first to celebrate *that* woman's graduation. She's lazier than an old recliner," Joi mused aloud. Pulling into her complex, she rounded the bend.

Getting home two hours after her day was scheduled to be over, was a sacrifice Joi was willing to make if it meant she got to start her vacation a day early. After raging through the office, refusing to fix what Caprice had broken, the Director decided to make the late hour worth her while. *"If you stay tonight and help us fix it, you can call off Friday as part of your Spring Break. Think about it. You'll have the entire day to yourself, and I promise I won't even call to ask a question. Just please stay. None of us know the programs as well as you."*

Guilt was the real deciding factor for Joi. When she glanced at the list of impacted students, she knew she wouldn't be able to sleep knowing they'd perceive their futures were in jeopardy. Already two dozen phone calls from those who received the notice regarding the blunder had been fielded by the office. Knowing she had done right by them would unburden her shoulders. Now with the next day off, she was freely singing her heart out to the current tune on the radio.

Slamming her car door, she finished off the piece she could no longer hear. "I'm about to diiiive in..." Her eyes squinting as she boldly went for the unreachable note.

Thinking she heard a buzz, Joi paused to look down into her purse. She glanced at her phone. The screen was blank, giving no indication of a missed call or text. She breathed a sigh of relief. For once, Joi hoped Gordon was giving too much of his time over to "that musty ole warehouse," he managed. Time would be her ally, as she was sure the carpet needed vacuuming, dishes needed to be washed, and the bed they shared was in need of a fresh set of linen.

"Everything's about to be spotless if it means he's going to sit me on that breakfast counter and spend the night devouring me. Or if the night becomes chilly, he can choose to roll our love around the carpet in front of the fireplace."

Anticipation of their entanglement caused her mouth to water. Her tongue snaked across her lips as she felt around in her bag for her house keys. Following the sound of the jingle, she was thankful she hadn't left them back at the office, which she was prone to do.

The couple was way overdue for a night of exploration. Two years into living together and they had already lost a piece of their groove. The past few weeks had been laced with disagreements, slammed doors, and silent nights over the lack of time they'd been able to spend together. Although, Joi was the one doing most of the protesting.

Nightly, she'd set dinner on the stove by six. The living room television would be stationed on ESPN and she'd be on the couch in her silk robe, dozing off as the hours without Gordon passed. Meanwhile, his dedication to his job at the fulfillment center had him pulling overnighters. Sitting in the window waiting for his car to pull into an open parking spot, proved to plummet her self-esteem and the more she pleasured herself in the bedroom, the less she looked forward to his touch. It seemed they were drowning in the never-ending cyclone of backs turned, forgotten smooches, and missed calls.

However, the call of Spring meant there was newness to come. Gordon's earlier voicemail implied he was looking to turn the tide. Halfheartedly, she believed him. He had made such vows in the past, resulting in them to be words he'd soon forget. Tonight though, she wouldn't let him charge change alone. She wouldn't doubt him but fall into submission. Taking in his words and whatever else he wanted her to swallow.

"My love is ready to come down," Joi hummed as she caught hold of her keyring.

The lavender lace bodice she purchased three weeks ago was finally about to have its night. Her normally long bouncing curls were going up in a bun and she'd smell of vanilla cream, wafting through his nostrils from the moment he'd enter the apartment. *Every inch of his six-foot six-inch peanut butter frame is about to have my fingers and tongue in full expedition mode.*

There'd be no bitter venom on her tongue. She'd talk with sugar, lay with grace, and take him into her, rejuvenating what it was to fall for each other.

"Oh, Mr. Thibodeau?" Her key still wedged in the lock; she listened for his reply. Voice dripping with intention, she called for Gordon again.

Joi peeked her head into the apartment. Overwhelmed with the scene, the only response she could muster was, "Wow!"

Floored at the set-up her juices were preparing to flow. It seemed Gordon had his own plans for tonight's rendezvous. The curtains were drawn closed. A single candle in the holder at the center of the coffee table was lit, illuminating the living space, creating enticing shadows and the mood for a lovers' tryst. The sexy sounds of old school, Babyface serenaded what she often referred to as her, Pelvic Goddess of Love. To her right, an unopened bottle of wine sat on the kitchen breakfast counter.

As the track moved on to Anita Baker's, *You Bring Me Joy*, she grinned. It was a song that was slightly before her time, but her mother sung it endlessly on Sundays after church, while Joi and her older sister, Camilla did their chores. As legend would have it, the number was playing overhead at the OB's office when they told Ms. Briar, she was having a girl. It was then she decided on the name, Joi Anita Briar, creating Joi's connection to the tune forevermore.

Joi turned to hang her blazer on the coat rack. She then toed out of her navy snakeskin pumps, and headed to the bedroom, making a pitstop in the kitchen to grab the wine bottle along the way. *Little does he know; I've got something for him too.*

A touch of rouge radiated through her cashew colored skin as she pictured what she'd look like once she squeezed into the purple lingerie and laid herself out for the taking. *He might think he's ready now, but I need to put on a show.* Fur arching the rim of the garment's bosom, her D-cups would be propped and ready for Gordon to feast.

Just as the song was switching to the next, she could hear the shower water running. Pictures of Gordon's tall, intensely defined, stark naked body filled her head. The way his muscles tensed when the heat touched his skin for the first time, was a view she'd take in time and time again. There were mornings when she ran late, watching his firmness cleanse beneath the waterfall.

Making the necessary detour, she crept toward the cracked door. Steam fogging the air, she spoke blindly. "You got room in there for one more?"

There was no response. She moved in closer. Swiping her hand along the glass, she saw that although the water had continued to run, the washroom was empty.

"Hmm. Strange. But I guess wine and steam wouldn't have mixed well anyway. Wouldn't want to pass out on him." She amused herself.

About faced, Joi placed her hand on the doorknob. It occurred to her; the music had stopped. Her heart quickening, she stood behind the door and peeked through its crack. There wasn't a body or a sound.

"This is ridiculous. We can't rebuild if I'm always trying to catch him. What if he's sprawled across the bed, in his boxers, waiting for me to hop on him? After this week of tension, I'm sure we can both use the release." Despite her assurance of being alone, her spoken thoughts were inaudible to anyone who wasn't standing beside her.

The music started up again. Melodic sounds of the group, Silk, begged to be freaked and vibrated the walls. Discreetly, she let herself out and walked across the carpet to the bedroom. Standing at the entryway, hand extended, ready to turn the knob and view her prize, she thought she heard a giggle. It was a spurt, light, almost undetectable. *I didn't hear... Wait, let me listen again.*

There was only the harmony of the singing quintet through the speakers. Relieved, she let out a deep breath. But then, there was a moan. And then another.

Her stomach was churning. Before she could take her next breath, a familiar voice purred, "Damn, Daddy. Let me hold it open for you."

Bile bubbled in her chest. "In our bedroom," Joi gasped in disbelief. Her eyes burned; head became light. She hadn't realized when she had moved forward, pushed the door open; until she stood facing Gordon with his torso pressed against and circling between, the salon-tanned, Botox injected rump of her absentee co-worker, Caprice. The girl's long, silky sheet of jet-black hair was clutched between his fingers.

What in the entire fu... Joi worked to restrain her emotions.

Pounding through her ears as if she was holding it captive, her heart clamored to be free of her chest. Her breathing remained evenly paced, however labored. Tears inched down her cheeks. Jaw clenched; her thoughts tumble weaved through her mind. *All her absences, his late nights...*

The lump in her throat was like a fist full of pebbles. Eyes bulged, she was inclined to scream, fight, dagger them both to death, but alas, she was paralyzed. Frozen by the cocktail of rage, she was confused, disappointed, but mostly, her heart was breaking. She could feel the pieces fracturing, preparing to shatter.

The sound of glass popping prompted Gordon to suspend his thrust. Quickly, he turned his head to see his girlfriend of three years, engine-red with anger, crushing the unopened bottle of wine with the one bare hand she held it in.

"Oh shit, Joi."

Caprice wiggled herself free of him. Scurrying to find her clothes, she did as she always did and started talking. "Joi, I'm sorry you had to find out this way," she sung, drawing out her words as though she was placing commas between each one.

"But you know, things happen for a reason. From the first time you introduced us, there was this..." she looked to the ceiling for an answer. "I don't know, magnetism?" Finding her underwear tossed over the back of the bedroom's armchair, she cautiously kept an eye on Joi as she plunged each of her legs through the lace openings.

Suddenly modest, Gordon wrapped the ecru bedsheet around his waist. He took notice of Joi's bleeding hand. "Joi? Put the bottle down. We can talk about this. That's a lot of blood you got there."

Subsequently finding her voice, she replied by growling, "Tell this bitch if she doesn't stop talking, and get the hell out of my sight, I'm going to shove every one of these shards down her throat!"

Burning flames lined Joi's vision. Boiling blood thickened her veins. Gordon flexed his shoulders, attempting to ready himself for the unpredictable. He had never experienced Joi with this amount of fury. There was no telling what move she'd make.

Gordon motioned his head for Caprice to leave. His eyes wouldn't abandon Joi as his focus. The intensity of her glare could levitate a mountain.

Taken aback by his agreement, Caprice blinked rapidly, waiting for him to come to his senses. However, Gordon wasn't reading her thoughts in this moment. Not like previous engagements when he read her interest in him, or when he picked up on the cue that said she wouldn't need much more than a suggestion to steal away with him at the apartment, in what had once been regarded as the temple he shared with Joi. Maybe he'd see to her feelings later. Right now, there was his used to be love, *ole pushover Joi*, dripping blood from her palms and craving a taste of his.

Unable to continue the still of contemplation, Joi opened her mouth. "You low-life, conniving, mother-fuc..." she shrieked as she lunged forward.

Her hands stretched in front of her like a vampire aiming to take hold of Gordon's chiseled neck, she choked back the rest of her verbal assault. There was an explosion happening in her cells and what she could make him feel took precedence over anything she had to say.

Calculating the danger Joi posed to them all, Caprice wizened up and made a b-line for the exit, bouncing breasts exposed. High tailing it out of the apartment, she had only been able to grab her teal, leather, studded moto jacket from off the back of the doorknob.

Gordon struggled to keep Joi's flailing arms under control. Once he thought he had her subdued, it seemed as if she'd magically untangle her way out of his grip and the battle would reignite with enhanced ferocity. He tried pulling her into his embrace, but that only succeeded in closing the gap between them enough for her to sink her teeth into his nipple, drawing the blood she needed to appease her.

Incapable of continuing to keep the words of her pain a secret, Joi swung, clawed, and shouted, "I hate you! You are selfish, vile, and I hate myself for loving you!" The least of which was more truth than she cared to admit.

As her barrage of fists pounded through Gordon's wrapped arms, four police officers came swarming into what was once the home Joi had dubbed, her sanctuary. Easily locating the commotion, the civil servants entered the bedroom where there was broken glass, spilled red wine across the off-white carpet, and Gordon; with scratches through his biceps and bloodstained prints on his cheek. He was failing to contain the fiery rainstorm of Joi's scorn.

For Joi, it was as if all the sound had been sucked out of the room. With her mouth ajar, pushing out her pain to the heavens, it seemed her voice had been muted. No matter the might behind her blows, they felt heavy, slow, and as she was hoisted in the air, they no longer had a place to land.

An officer had slipped his arms around Joi's waist, carrying her out of the apartment. Continuously swinging, it wasn't until she was out in the lot, being led into the backseat of a squad car when she let her fists fall to her side. Other than losing her father to a heart attack twenty-two years ago, Thursday, March 14th was now registering as the worst day of her life. Saltwater drenched her face. She wondered if this agony would ever be consolable.

A LACK OF *appetite*

"Nile, why would you actually request to be reassigned here? Of all the places you could've chosen with your tenure, you chose the hood. Policeman are the actual targets around here, if you haven't noticed."

Definitely not the noise I want this bedroom to be filled with. The sound of Liana's whining ripped through Nile's senses. His nerves cringed and the bridge of his nose was starting to ache. Whenever Liana was of an opposing opinion, she'd drag her words as though she had the ability to shift his stance. Unbeknownst to her, over the past few weeks, Nile had been questioning why he continued to bed her. This morning would be no different. *It's not like I could question her beauty. No one can, really. Her features are phenomenal. And honestly, she isn't just good looks. She does have valid points to back up whatever corner of the room she's standing for in the moment, but it's so damn irritating that she relies on perking her tits and babying her voice to get me to hear her. Grow up, already.*

With arms folded across her breasts, Liana, pursed her lips as she sat up in Nile's king-sized platform bed. Bronzed skin revealing the heat of her crimson undertone, she huffed. "It's like you are hell bent on putting your life in danger. It's ridiculous." She pouted.

Sitting on the cushioned bench at the foot of the bed, Nile remained unmoved as he slid into the legs of his uniform. "Liana, I'm tired of going through this with you. I am an officer of the law. What job did you think I signed up for?" He stood to buckle. Despite being strapped in his undershirt, he was giving her a full view of the sculptured back she once likened to a chocolate covered museum statue.

"If I'm going to protect and serve, why wouldn't I want to do so for my own people? It's actually amazing to me that you're not on board with this," he reasoned as he rechecked his cell phone.

Still open an taking over the screen, was the email notification detailing the granting of his solicited assignment. However, his excitement had withered. *Sad how this girl could actually dry up an ocean with all her salt.*

"Because it's freaking dangerous," Liana exclaimed. A blanket of brunette tresses falling to her shoulders, she puffed, blowing a few of the loose strands away from her face.

By any man's account, Liana's sexual prowess was undeniable. Four nights a week at the gym, kept her buttocks lifted, her abs flat, and her melon breasts perked. Attending the newly renovated health club was strategic on her part though. After a night of lovemaking, she confessed her true intention.

If she had it her way, Liana wouldn't revisit the old neighborhood but once a year to see her grandmother. But last Christmas when she was forced to stop at the Liquor Store to pick up her Uncle Larry's holiday taste, she was pleasantly surprised by whom she'd retell as a smoldering, Hershey officer, standing behind her. She boasted his skin was like the finest of chocolates. Smooth and primed for eating. Feeling the heat of his presence heating up her rear, her organs throbbed, immediately concluding he was meant to be hers. Her intuition told her the handsome man was trying his best to keep his attention off of her, as a means of politeness. He was respectful and needed a sign okaying an approach. Subtly, she turned to him and smiled. However, despite his glimpse of her full lips and perfectly stacked assets, he didn't speak, didn't chase her down, and he didn't look twice before he sped away to his own destination.

A few more drop-ins, checking on Granny's health, led Liana to find Nile's stress-reliever workouts were being conducted at the gym behind the old Community Center. Once she joined, she made it her mission to give him something to ogle. After nineteen days, and six instances of eye contact with only nods of hello between them, she threw caution to the wind and asked for his number.

Although flattered, Nile was hesitant to let Liana into his space. His experience with women hadn't been the greatest. Most of those he came across, couldn't handle the anxiety of his profession. Each fail was disappointing, but he did his best to be understanding. *No one wants to imagine someone they care about taking a bullet in the midst of an altercation. Not to mention the hardship of being out with a man clothed in a uniform that could make him public enemy number one, depending on who's present. Still, it'd be nice to have a family. Someone who looked for me to come home but supported my duty on these streets.*

Nile dated Liana for six weeks before he invited her inside his townhome. Whenever he'd take her out to eat, he'd listen to her talk, pondering how much trouble she'd be. Her opinions were strong and that was what he liked most about her. She paid attention to what was going on around her and processed it. But then he started to notice her half-truths and willingness to misrepresent information when it was convenient. Tracking him down to the gym was cute at first, but once she confessed, he realized she might not have cared as much for her grandmother as she presented. *Savage.* He toiled with deciding if he was complimented or slightly turned off by her brand of resolve.

As she continued her tirade over his new field assignment, her voice was landing on his ears as a warped blabbering. He asked himself, *why did I let her in again? Well, let's not ask stupid questions, shall we? It was because with all that ass wagging and sexual innuendos, I needed to know what she felt like.*

But the moment she felt his girth between her thighs, she was determined to slow grind her way into locking him in as hers. Which, at first Nile thought he could get on board with. Until she revealed her lack of faith in the rehabilitation projects that had been going on around the neighborhood. She had no hope for the very same people he was trying to build a rapport with. The kids he mentored at the gym would be met with her scowl and dismissal. When he'd point out new construction for coming businesses, she'd roll her eyes, purse her lips, and then abruptly change the subject. A vixen's body was a pleasure to fondle, but her inability to uplift anyone not looking back at her in the mirror, dulled his attraction. Yet, she'd hold on. Choosing not to complain about their dates moving from weekly to every other, she'd make sure whatever he was thinking would be cast aside the moment he took in her curves.

Liana's toned thighs slipped from beneath the tussled bedsheets. She squirmed off of the bed. Her only dressing, the golden thong Nile had moved aside the night before, she stood before him, encouraging her lover to give her a once-over. She hung her head, allowing her eyes to travel down to her pelvis as if he needed guidance to where she wanted him to keep focus.

Looking back up into his glare, and biting down on her bottom lip, she sauntered closer. Determining a soapbox would be coming right along with her, Nile held his breath. She poked her lip out while focusing on his brawn.

"Where's the solidarity when something happens to you, baby? The mere fact that you care so much is admirable, but these people don't deserve to have your life. What will become of me without you?"

He squeezed his eyes shut. *This is what you get for thinking with your little man.* Upon the fluttering of his lids, he prayed he'd be able to say what was needed without shouting, and although it was a longshot, without having to watch the dripping of her tears.

"These people, Liana? You talk like you didn't grow up half a block from a round-the-way bodega. These people are your family.

Your freaking grandmother still lives here. The daughters and sons of the same citizens you shared your childhood with attend these schools. And why are you writing my death sentence? The whole point is to reshape, rectify, and redefine the relationship between the force and the people we're supposed to protect. Get us all on the same side."

She slid her arms around his waist. "First, you sound like a rally pamphlet. Second, don't take it that way. I'm just saying they are out here selling drugs to each other, stealing from one another, and shooting up the properties the elders struggled to purchase. When you have no other choice but to do your job and lock away the ingrates you care so much about, then what? Who will you be to them? Remember that officer who was shot in New York? The guy who did it travelled from another state just to take retaliation on anyone who was wearing the uniform. He didn't care who it was, what they believed, or the mourning that would come on the heels of it. All they will see you as, is someone who is choosing blue over Black or whatever it is, they say. Certainly not the superhero you picture yourself to be. I just can't let you give yourself over to such a futile cause." She rested her head at the top of his torso.

Nile sighed. *This is probably going to hurt her more than I want it to.* One limb at a time, he peeled her off of him. "Li, this won't work. We're just too different."

"What?" Her head jerked back.

Pupils darting from side to side, she tried to search his expressionless face for clarity. She was stunned. No one had ever ended things with her before. Mentally reviewing the details of her past relationships, it had always been her deciding situations needed to come to an end. Not once in her recollection had anyone willingly walked away from her. What Nile was proposing was not only foreign, but utterly ridiculous.

"We can't keep going on like this. Everything with you is negative if it isn't your ideal picture of running off into the sunset and away from everything you come from. I don't even know what took me so long to see it. Or maybe I did, and just refused to admit it."

Liana chuckled. Pushing her hair behind her ear, purposely exposing her diamond studs, she popped her hip. "Really? Must you be so dramatic? Because I'm trying to keep you safe you have to sling insults at me? You're tripping for real." She looked on as he grabbed his badge from the onyx stained armoire drawer.

Completing his suit-up with a City of Wilmington, shoulder shielded, short-sleeved button down and tucking it in, he threw the bit of explanation that he was compelled to spare, over his shoulder. "Foundationally, we aren't on the same page. The effort to explain to you who I am and what I'm hitting for, I don't have time for today." Plucking her brassiere from the middle dresser drawer knob, he turned to walk it over to her.

Appalled, Liana rushed into him with her arms swinging, aimlessly. "Screw you, Nile! How dare you fault me for my truth!"

Before she could land any one of her hurled, closed fisted disappointments against his chest, he caught her wrists. He held her still. "Nor can you fight me for mine. For almost four months we've enjoyed each other, but you're some other man's dream. There's a dude out there who will kiss the ground you walk on, share your sentiments, and not choose to live the kind of life that has you full of worry. It's best we let it go before one of us falls in love." *This is truly my fault. Something told me to leave her alone. I didn't listen to my gut and now she's going to hate me.*

His last spoken sentence settling into her hearing, her rage multiplied. "Who do you think I am?" she screeched.

I'm an ass. My mother raised an ass. No, don't tell her that. This has nothing to do with my mother or my father for that matter. My hormones were hungry and now I'm acting like she's the one whose poison. Much repentance needs to happen.

"I'm not just some fly by night call girl you can put out after you've had enough fun." Her voice trembling, she worked to gather herself.

Then as meek as the way she touched his cheek during the afterglow of their midnight passion, she continued, "You were falling, Nile. I know you. There's no way you can tell me you weren't. It hasn't even been a full three hours since we…"

He released her. "I won't insult you by telling you I don't care for you. We both know that's not real. But from the way this conversation is going down, you really don't know me. This transfer is literally the whole reason I entered the Academy. For this very opportunity."

Defeated, she dropped her hands. Head hung and all out of protests, she snatched her bra. Hastening to grab her mahogany bodycon dress from the spot on the carpet where he had been eager to spring her from it, she attempted to swallow the tears that were threatening to embarrass her further. Scrunching her nose, mid-reach, she stared at the dress a moment. It lay rumpled like the wave of emotions rippling through the room. She'd have to armor herself in it and pretend there wasn't a stepped-on heart beneath it.

Nile watched as the woman he woke up to, squeezed herself back into last night's attire. As much as he wanted to wrap his arms around her, whisper his apologies, he knew he couldn't. Because none of it would change the need to say goodbye.

DECAFFEinated

"Joi, pick up!"

The cell phone shouted from beneath the covers. It was Thursday, the hardest for Joi to force herself out of a semi-decent slumber. Despite the comforting pink silk belted across her lids, keeping her eyes closed at night was a concentrated effort. However, without fail, once the digits on the cable box ticked the striking of the four o'clock hour, she'd fall into the deep; away from her memories and into the console of darkness. Required to rise only three hours later was tedious, but on Thursdays it felt devastating. Another shout from her cellular would remind her it was that time.

"Noooo," Joi moaned at the repetitive demand.

Agreeing to give her sister, Camilla access to record her own ringtone was high on Joi's current running list of life mistakes. Feeling around for the screaming device, she was desperate to keep her eyes closed. But gripping nothing but the eight hundred thread count sheet provided her with yet another miss. She sighed in exasperation.

"Fine!" She ripped the eye mask from her face and flung it across the room. Immediately spotting the phone, she grabbed it, pressing onto the screen.

"Took you long enough, Briar," Camilla blared. She popped her gum.

"Must you call me by our last name? It's not even yours anymore. You've been a Hamilton for like ten years now. It's super annoying. We're not in the military. And do you have to file your nails every morning?" The November chill crisping against the bedroom window reminded her of the cold world, awaiting her entry.

"How you know that's what I'm doing? I swear you need to go on one of them talent shows or something and tell 'em about your bat ears. Oh wait, you can't make no money from that, can you?"

Camilla tilted her head as she held the phone between her ear and shoulder. Rolling her eyes, she set to continue her habitual filing. She and Joi were thirteen months apart, but their outlooks on love and the chasing of dreams would sometimes seem to separate them by generations. There wasn't a thing that would stop Camilla from pursuing the life she wanted, regardless of what heavy emotions she was dealing with. Back when she swaggered through the halls of her High School, she was determined to keep her heart off of her sleeve. It was that very same persona that she credited for leading her to her diamond in the rough. Her husband, Terrence was once an influential figure in the city's drug game. When he had been charged for his crimes, a technicality prevented him from doing the promised quarter century in prison. Once given a second chance with the world at his feet, he, Camilla, and the rest of their family made a plan to keep his hands clean. He never looked back. However, Joi, unlike her name, was frightfully fading into depression since her last break up.

"Get your beautiful self up and go to work. I'm already dressed. You're making me late and there is money that begs to be made. Besides, you can't find your Prince laying up in the bed all day. That comes after you find him," Camilla snickered.

"Constantly, you're yapping about some damn Prince that doesn't exist. Can't you just leave me alone and let me crawl back into bed?" Although she wanted to stay put, Joi knew she couldn't. She swung her legs over the side of her plush mattress.

"You're my baby sister. Ain't no leaving you alone." Pausing her file, Camilla rested her fist on her hip, per her usual stance.

Rarely did it take long for her to get fed up with her baby sister. She contemplated if she'd have to remove her earrings. The call was panning out to be longer than the two minutes she calculated.

"Seriously? You've barely got me by a year, and you act like you're older than Mama. Besides, don't you have your own baby to attend to?" Joi shuffled toward the bathroom.

"Kitty is already on the bus and at five years old, she stopped being more baby than you. Matter of fact, just the other day your niece, little Miss Katoi, asked why her Auntie Joi is so sad. Now how am I supposed to explain to an eight-year-old that her favorite person is out here moping around over *he who shall not be named*, despite splitting up four months ago? You should've let Terrence press him. It might've made you feel better."

Joi recalled the scene like it was yesterday.

Camilla and Terrence spared no time coming to retrieve her from the police station. Whom they referred to as Uncle Bruce, their mother's longtime "friend," phoned Camilla, asking her to drop whatever she was doing and get down to the precinct. As a retired police Sargent, he had comrades on the inside looking out for the girls. Neither of the sisters knew which were Bruce's eyes and ears, but they had always felt protected. His own secret society, they called it.

Terrence was in the driver's seat. His Yankee baseball hat cocked to the side, he glanced at Joi through the rearview mirror. "How you want to handle this guy?"

Camilla was riding shotgun. She chewed the side of her cheek, visibly pissed at what transpired between Joi and Gordon. As children she fought each and every one of Joi's battles. There wasn't one Joi could recall Camilla losing. If she wasn't the victor of one round, she'd come back time after time until it had been settled to her liking.

As much as their mother loved the both of them, Camilla loved Joi just as much. From the moment she was brought home from the hospital, Joi had become Camilla's most loved relative. There was no harm against her sister that wasn't taken personally. And where Camilla was concerned, that meant Terrence needed to get himself involved as well. It had become the nature of things. He'd go to the depths of space if it meant he would right whatever Camilla declared wrong. Because she was aware of his position when it came to her, she would usually keep drama far off of his radar. But this was different. For her sister, her "Baby Cute," this pain was gut-wrenching, life changing, and she didn't know how else to alleviate it.

Joi deliberated for several minutes. Although she was tempted, she concluded that she couldn't let Terrence do what she was certain he would. Gordon wouldn't just be harmed. He'd be tortured and instead of left for dead, he'd be purposely sentenced to live, ensuring he'd suffer through whatever permanent scar Terrence had decided was his justice. But Gordon had convoluted pride. Too proud to admit that he deserved to be showered by hell fire for how he handled her, he'd need revenge in the form of telling his tale to the authorities and having Terrence face unfathomable years behind bars. Joi wouldn't have been able to handle that kind of weight on her conscious. Nor could she concede to handing Gordon that type of power.

"Take me home. Let karma ravage him." As she stared of the backseat window, she remained silent, but her pain continued to cry out.

Yanking herself from the memory, Joi quipped, "It's been seven and a half months since Gordon and I separated, but I see your point."

Five months of working in the financial aid office of Trailblazer College hadn't seemed to make the days get any easier. Joi thought for sure, switching offices would mitigate her angst. But the constant explanation of school benefits and the sob stories she couldn't remedy left her feeling as though the Universe was some crazy ass bitch, running her down, waving the repercussions left over from a previous existence.

She exhaled while dotting her automatic toothbrush with toothpaste. Avoiding staring at her reflection in the mirror, Joi focused on her breathing. It was time to face the next twenty-four hours.

"Okay, I'm up for real now, Milla. Don't be late for work. Thank you for setting me straight. And for Katoi, I will seize the day and leave my heart out of it."

"Well I don't know if we are asking all that. Only for you to know that the end of that man's love ain't the end of you. I just want you to love yourself enough to open up to the fullness of real love. To bathe in it. Bask in it. Let it emanate from your soul. Have children with it. Then bless the world with it."

Camilla's words were getting caught in her throat. On the brink of tears, she fanned her burning eyes. Because Camilla Briar-Hamilton was the epitome of theatrical.

Still, the memory of how Gordon Thibodeau basically squatted and took a dump all over her sister's heart was enough to make her search for him and kill him herself. Make no mistake, her husband would be fully on board at the slightest signal of a need to follow through. Together, they'd make a convincing case to Mama Briar and Uncle Bruce, requiring the family heads to turn the other cheek as though they were never aware of what was happening.

"You know what?" The dramatic pause was a friend that visited many of the sisters' conversations. "Let me stop before I end up killing *my* morning. Kisses, my sweet Joi. Call me if you need anything."

Ending the call, Joi continued her routine. After brushing her teeth, she'd spend five minutes in the steamiest of showers, attempting to scrub away the loath she had for daytime hours. But five minutes, she one day figured out, was all she could stand. If she stayed a sixth, her imagination would run wild, picturing Gordon's hands and lips all over Caprice, the woman he had chosen to settle for. Embarrassment would swivel around in her abdomen, at times, lurching up into her esophagus. The girl was barely twenty-three. Still, the moment Gordon walked in for an impromptu lunch date with Joi, the salaciousness was piqued. Batting her lashes, Caprice swooned as he introduced himself. Oblivious to Gordon's returned interest, Joi laughed it off as a student's cute little crush. Afterall, what would a thirty-five-year-old man see in such a green conquest? *Every damn thang, apparently.*

With an oversized towel secured around her frame; Joi creamed her butter pecan breasts with banana scented cocoa butter. It was her favorite of the concoctions Camilla sold. She inhaled, taking in the aroma. Exhaling, she was beginning to feel better prepped for the day ahead. *You are joy, you are power, you will rise to greatness.*

"Today will be unlike any other. I will not just go through the motions. I will speak as if I have been resurrected," she asserted aloud, while spreading the scent throughout the rest of her body. Scoping the closet, then deciding on a hunter green wool wrap dress, she continued to affirm, "Gordon has stolen my yesterdays, but I will not hand him today. Besides, if I want to keep Camilla out of prison, I need to get it together. Terrence doesn't need to catch any cases behind my stupid heartbreak or my sworn protector's sword either." Joi chuckled to herself.

"Ridiculous, aren't I? That's truly how I'm behaving. If Gordon showed up today with apologies on his breath and regret in his heart, I would turn him away without a second thought. But by God, I tell you, shame is one hell of a bullet. Thank goodness for morning slices of chocolate cake. Soon as I get to Sweet Thangs, all will feel right with the world."

CHOCOLATE cake

Temperatures had fallen to twenty-five degrees on average everyday this first week of November. As Nile whipped the squad car around the bend, he had been thinking about the previous night's dinner with his parents. *"You're coming up on thirty-five, Nile. I get you younger folks are waiting before having children, but goodness, dear will we be grandparents in our lifetime?"*

His mother's question was reverberating through his head. As the only child, continuing the Ledger family name was on him as far as Stephanie and Grady Ledger were concerned. Was there a slew of male cousins on his father's side who had succeeded in seeding what seemed like a quarter of the globe? Absolutely. But no, the elder Mr. Ledger needed his branch to bear fruit and Mrs. Ledger was in total agreeance.

After forty years of marriage, the aging couple were still as much in love as year three, if you let Stephanie Ledger tell it. *"The first two years took some adjusting."* She'd smile, knowingly as she cupped the cheek of her love's smooth, baby-bottom-like, midnight skin. Grady Ledger would lean in and plant a gentle kiss to her mocha forehead, undoubtedly thanking her for whatever angelic forgiveness she had bestowed upon him in the past.

Nile considered their interaction. The way his mother pursed her lips when she was sharing the "realness" of their union, he could detect there was a storm his parents had battled, maybe even struggled to survive. But when the woman's eyes met her beau's, she'd continue with a softness that said he had more than made up for it over time. Recalling her son's presence across the dining room table, yet unable to look away from her King, she'd gift Nile her prayer. *"My hope is, one day you'll find the love you're willing to work for, my son. Because when you do, it will fill you, ground you, and elevate you."*

Grinning as though he was under a spell, Nile's father was sure to add, *"All at the same damn time."*

Making a right into what was once an abandoned field of a parking lot and veering to the left, Nile searched for an empty spot. *No surprise, everyone's out in this cold trying to get some heat from Sweet Thangs. By the size of these morning crowds, they should think about opening up another location in a minute.*

Getting his mind right, before the call of duty this morning, would take something hot and laced with extra caffeine. Silencing the squad car engine, he snatched the remote speaker from the passenger seat and clipped it to his lapel. He heard the static of an incoming.

"Officer Ledger, would your fine chocolate self, do me a favor and grab me a Coconut Hot Cocoa on your way in?" Sheryl, the precinct dispatcher radioed.

She had him timed, but he accepted her monitoring as no bother. Admittedly, knowing that someone on the force knew how he moved during his early hours made him feel as though not having a partner didn't mean he was without back-up. And he liked that the senior woman took him personal. On several occasions she referred to him as her adopted nephew.

Nile hadn't had a steady partner since being transferred to what the department referred to as, Grade D. The shootings, inconsolable grandmothers hovering over bodies on the pavement, and living room floor overdoses throughout the sixty-block radius, was enough to make anyone put in for early retirement. But this was where he preferred to be. Where he was needed and if they let him, where he could be part of the healing.

A harmless flirt, Sheryl had been with the unit for close to thirty years. After all she had seen and heard, if all she needed was a hot cocoa to make her day, then as far as Nile was concerned, every officer in the tri-state should spare the time to bring her one. Squeezing the buttons at either side of the speaker attached to his collar, he replied "With pleasure. Once I tell her it's for you, she'll make it a double."

From the moment he rose from the car, the wind smacked against his jaw. The fragrance of heated chocolate swirled with the intoxicating scent of melted caramel floated through his nostrils. Everyone from high schoolers to Business District execs braved frigid pandemonium in order to be served at this six-month old, pink and powder blue shop. In this moment, Nile was the same as anyone else, damn near skipping to get a dose straight from the source, the "Sunrise Sugar Rush," of Sweet Thangs.

A rarity in the neighborhood, Sweet Thangs was a boutique baker's cafe off of New Castle Avenue. Since its inception, by seven thirty in the morning, it was a buzzing madhouse. The makeshift double lines trailed out of the plexiglass doors and spilled out into the parking area. A soft contrast to the city's dreary landscape, it seemed as if overnight the confectionary had become the area's preferred rest stop for its, "Sunrise Sugar Rush." No one could blame themselves for craving the dream state indulgence. The shop's visionary, Anada Moore, was gifted when it came to baked goods, and the magic she conjured with flavors and expresso had Nile becoming a non-paid spokesperson at the precinct for her brand.

Once he stepped inside, he tried keeping to the rear. Per usual, patrons cleared a way for him, respecting his uniform, to glide to the front counter. Doing his best to remain gracious, he thanked them but kept his positioning. They all needed their fix as much as he did.

"Okay who's got the Vanilla Caramel Cream Prep, Large?" Anada shouted out into the crowd.

Several teenage girls bustled to the front, nearly knocking over an elderly, disheveled man. Nile tilted his head, believing he had seen the jittered brother panhandling the night before. Recognizing there was law enforcement present, the girls persisted in their apologies. However, it didn't stop one from grabbing her cup and dashing out of the door with claims of almost missing her bus. The man migrated off to the side, careful not to continue to become a nuisance to anyone else.

Anada made eye contact with Nile. She nodded her greeting and then proceeded to scan the wave of awaiting customers, searching for a who or perhaps a what. A slow shake of her head told him exactly what she was seeking. He grinned. *Still on the hunt, I see.*

Acknowledging the entrepreneur as a prominent community member, Nile had befriended Anada over the past few months. He'd stop in during quiet afternoons, ordering the Lime Dark Brownie Crumble. It didn't take long for her staff of two to persuade him to be the Guinea pig for new coffee and treat flavor creations. Often, Anada would note that Nile's demeanor reminded her of her husband, Dylan, when he was in his youth. *"Charming and seemingly unaware of his allure, Dylan, like you, made for good company. Still does. Generous too. In fact, I've already talked to Dylan about inviting you over for dinner. However, Dylan wants to be the one to extend the invite. So, you'll have to wait for eternity or something like that."*

Anissa, the Assistant Manager would chime in with a wave of her hand. *"He keeps popping in during the evening to kiss his wife and grab his own bit of her sugary sweetness. Then he has a look around, looking for you like you camp out here. Doesn't matter how many times she advises him that you work the early morning shift and sporadically join us for afternoon breaks. But you know, he's old and in his routine."* Waving her hand, she'd continue, *"Promising to make it* over in the AM only to do the same doggone thing each time. He sure remembers to grab Ms. Anada's butt, though."

Jumping to her husband's defense, Anada would playfully poke Anissa about calling her husband old when he had yet to turn fifty. She was nearing the age herself and didn't appreciate being bucketed into the category of those who were stubborn and forgetful. They'd somehow allow the conversation to trail into talks about Nile's intention to heal the relationships between the force and those he swore to protect. Another reason why Anada thought Dylan would be fond of the young policeman.

Definitely the big sister type, Anada was always skipping through her mental rolodex to find someone to hook Nile up with. Once he confided in her his break-up with Liana, she was on a tunnel-vision mission to get him hitched. But it wasn't just her. Anissa and the other young woman she employed, Vashti, were in on it too. On top of it all, Anissa was Sheryl's niece and recruited her for the pursuit as well. It was a whole woman gang. Jokingly, Nile often referred to them as his personal street team. Several times, he had to remind them he wasn't interested in anyone who had just earned the privilege of drinking or who believed themselves to be social media famous. After every search where there was no one they'd all agree upon, Anada would sigh in disappointment and disbelief. *"Why, just yesterday, Mrs. Creole said she'd lie about her sixty years on this earth if it meant she could steal you away for sixty minutes. And yet we can't seem to find you a nice woman to at least take on a date. We're failing you, dear."* She'd then laugh at the absurdity of the lack of options.

Going over their past conversations in his head, Nile shook his head. One of his father's sayings, circled through his head. *There is no fail where there's genuine care, laughs, and a hot pot of coffee.*

At night, after a long day of pat-downs, lectures, and cruise patrols, Nile would rather reflect on the women's playful yet insistent work to find him the other half, they decided he needed. Stationed in front of the television, watching anything but the news, he'd pick up the phone to scroll through his social media timelines. All his "bros" it seemed, were with their treasured others. Some were welcoming children while others were readying themselves to send wedding invitations. His father's prophetic voice constantly based through his thoughts. *She's coming, son. You're a good man, much better than I raised you to be. Don't worry about your mother and her need to call herself a grandmother. Even though I put her up to it. But you know, you only have to plant a seed with that woman. I've watched you and the choices you make are noble. The right woman is going to come along and welcome all that love you've got waiting to spill. I know you say you don't need it and you're okay with it. But once you find it, you won't know how you lived without it.*

Still, Nile considered it plausible to think there may not be one to fit the bill. And yet, he was compelled to contemplate what it was he might've desired. *A woman who had spent some time getting to know her confidence, would be a prize-winning find. One who didn't need to pretend she liked what I like or solicited the attention of every man with his tongue out, in order to provoke a reaction from me.*

He wasn't oblivious to the anxiety that came with dating a police officer. The uniform drew a lot of attention. Some naughty and some not so nice. And Nile found it to be an energy sucking endeavor to spend his time continually consoling fears or managing egos. For now, though, he determined all he needed, was a large cup of joe.

After adding a bit of vanilla cream into the branded, insulated cup before her, Anada stirred milky liquid in with the brewed coffee and then added in two shots of piping expresso. From a squeeze bottle, she topped it off with her unique melted caramel creation. She placed her signature, teal plastic lid atop and motioned for Nile to come forward.

"The six-foot-four, husky, roasted chestnut, statuesque man, isn't just here to survey, I see. This sexy bit of chocolate actually drinks coffee like he ain't the best bit of dark roast." A medium brown, double breasted woman snickered into the crowd. She licked her lips, causing a clique of earshot adolescents to giggle.

Receiving the steaming vessel, Nile handed it to the homely man who had almost lost his footing earlier. "Here, you take this one. The day is long, and I've got time this morning."

The man's smile revealed missing teeth, but a lightened load. "A standup servant of the law; would you look at that. There's still hope. Bless you, young man," he slurred.

Nile ushered him out and watched as he stumbled out of the parking lot. He had an inkling the kind officer was standing watch. He turned to wave once he found his path along the sidewalk. Satisfied with the fellow's assurance of being okay, Nile pulled the handle on the shop's door, pausing to make a mental note to add a box of Pineapple Right-Side Cake Donuts, to his tab.

There was a light tap to his shoulder. "Excuse me, are you going in?"

Melodizing through his hearing, the stranger's voice reminded Nile of a sultry blues singer, gracing the stage of a smoky lounge. Finding it difficult not to get lost in a thoughtful dissertation about how soul-freeing her voice was, he stepped back to see a woman who'd only given her side profile to him. Large, thick, and fluffy curls beneath her beige tam, flowed down to her shoulders. She continued to look away. At least a foot shorter than him, he instantly felt the need to pull her into his chest. Other than a peeking smile though, her face was still a mystery.

Upon Nile's return inside, he caught a glimpse of Anada's approving glare. She tapped Anissa who then tapped Vashti and they all lit up as though they were staring at a giant-sized Christmas tree. His attention, however, was quickly returned to the angel with no name.

As the intriguing woman took her place on the line, Nile's heartrate quickened. Never had he been so captivated with just a voice and piece of an image. He deliberated over what he would say to her. *What's your name? No, I can't just come right out and ask that. I'm a friggin' cop. She'll think she did something wrong. But damn, maybe she did, 'cause I'm just gawking at her like a creep.*

Apparently reading Nile's mind, Anada's head motioned to Anissa and then to him. Catching on, Anissa smirked and then nudged Vashti. *This must be what it's like to have sisters.* The three of them whizzed through the orders only to take their time with his "fair lady's" request.

"A slice of Thursday Thrive Chocolate Cake, please." Her preference was that of a child's but her tone, Nile couldn't deny, was laced with mature femininity.

"Good morning, Miss Joi," Anada greeted. She made it her business to know the names of each of her frequent visitors. But the way she softened her speech, it was as if she was being purposely gentle. "Vashti will grab the new batch off the kitchen counter," she advised while simultaneously instructing Vashti.

Anissa punched the total in on the cash register then collected the four dollars from the pleasant beauty. Nile took note of how her eyes smiled at this, "Joi," as well. Something about the woman had them being delicate and he had a feeling it wasn't strictly because he had fully sat the thought of her on his radar.

"No rush," Joi replied as she stepped off to the side. Clutching her wallet, it seemed she was avoiding Nile's glare.

"You say that every morning, Momma. Either you've got the best job in the world or the absolute worst. You're never in a hurry to get there," Anissa gleefully observed.

Joi sighed. "If you only knew, honey. This cake is about the only thing that keeps me friendly on a day like today."

While they awaited Vashti's presentation, Anissa brought Nile his custom cup of jolt over to him and added Sheryl's too. "Tell my Aunt Sheryl, I'll be over for Bingo tonight." Gathering his attention was still on the beauty whose name was apparently roaming the halls of his mind, she asked through gritted teeth, "Donuts too, right? I'm trying to buy you some time here, but you're not making a move. Get them balls swinging, my man."

Without Nile's verbal reply, Anissa was gone back behind the counter. A master multi-tasker, she was readying his baker's dozen along with dispersing the single orders of Cherry Cocoa Donuts to the thinning mass. Furrowing her brow, she looked up, using her glare to direct him.

Taking his cue, Nile stepped over to where Joi was leaning against the edge of one of the dine-in tables. "At ten minutes to eight you're having chocolate cake?" Sounding much different than he planned, he was perturbed by his baritone inquisition. *She's probably asking herself, "Who is this clown sounding like a school Principal?" Why did I sound so forceful? Could I not think of anything else to say? She won't even face me.* He shifted his weight.

Joi smiled, seemingly to herself. Keeping her focus on her calf high, taupe suede boots, she was reluctant to answer. But then she countered, "Sometimes you need dessert in the morning." Finally, lifting her head, she met his gaze.

Time became an indescribable, slow-moving, cosmic force of existence the instant she looked at him. All the years his father tried to capture in words what it was he felt at the first sight of his future wife's face, Nile now suddenly comprehended. *Although, I guess I've got one up on you, Pop. She had me over here with sweaty palms off a glimpse of her profile. And now that she's given me her face, my God...* Her dark browns took hold of him like it was his first meeting with daybreak; rising and full of the promise of light.

Morning commuters busied out, carrying on their chase for timeliness. Nile quietly stood beside Joi, contemplating how to proceed. Her hard to hide hips were draped beneath layers of wool between her tan ankle length peacoat and her hunter green dress. *Damn, she's fine.* Shining through the windows, the sun glistened over her sugar cone skin, highlighting her cheekbones as if it were directing him where to kiss. He waited for another sound to come from her lips, another quip or maybe an introduction. However, his luck would not come easy.

Anissa giggled. "Let me find out the crush has got his tongue. And all this time we thought his only problem was options," she teased. It was intended to be an inner thought, but Anissa, as sweet as she was, had no clue how to whisper. Lucky for her, she didn't intend to live a life of crime.

As Vashti carefully carried the batch of Chocolate Thursday Thrive Cake slices to the back counter, Anissa quickened to her side. "Ms. Anada gave you permission to take the first cut, didn't she," she quizzed.

Grinning like a Cheshire Cat, Vashti replied, "Please don't shake your head. I already hate that I'm this easy."

Anissa matched her presumed giddy. "I for one, love that you are. Now make sure you add the special bow to Joi's piece. Nile's over there hovering like a lovesick puppy. Maybe it'll give him something to ask about. Poor man needs all the help he can get."

Shyly, Joi dipped her head, perusing what selection the glass casing beneath the counter held for the day. It had been a while since she'd ordered anything to send to her mother's house. Bruce was the lover of treats over there and at times Joi would send something over to allow her mama less guilt about not succumbing to his sweet tooth during the week. She could feel Nile watching her movements. The butterflies in her tummy fluttered around in hysteria, wondering if he'd say anything else.

Meanwhile, Nile was trying to figure out the situation. He knew why the baker's crew always looked out for him. Over time they had become akin to family. But now, they were making a fuss over Joi and he was trying to establish why. Was she one of Anada's relatives? A celebrity he was unaware of? Daughter of an investor or local Congressman?

Vashti stood, her head peeking over the countertop, to find Joi's agreeable smile, awaiting her regular order. "Sorry I took so long. I know you have to get to work."

"Maybe you should give her two slices, for her inconvenience," Nile chimed.

Each of the women had raised eyebrows. He was well aware that he was doing a poor job at selecting the right words to gain entry to the world of Joi. After all the talks the girls had about hooking him up, he hoped they'd realize now would be the perfect time to get activated.

"Everything good over at the college, Ms. Joi? I plan to re-enroll at Trailblazer next semester." Vashti had perceived Nile's anguish and decided to step in.

Joi had moved closer to Vashti's preparations. Although there was much less of an audience now, Vashti added volume to the conversation, easing Nile's eavesdropping efforts. With the mass thinning, she was careful not to shout too loud as not to be overt.

Well played, baby sis.

"We'd love to have you back. Let me know if there's anything I can do to make the process easier. You remember where my new office is?" Joi asked while accepting her package, then burying her nose in the bag, allowing the aroma to drift through her senses. Now facing the remainder of the day was truly possible. The fragrance alone would get her through her commute and once she got a taste of her fix, whatever difficulties she foresaw would become easy enough hurdles to jump. Although, the etched memory of the rousing man gaping at her would definitely contribute to easing any pent-up frustrations.

"First floor, across from the Bursar's office, but head to the back." Vashti glanced back over at Nile's watchful eyes.

With Vashti's indiscreet motions, Joi craned her neck. She came face to face with him, dark-eyed, broad shouldered, and seemingly awestricken with her beauty. Up until now she was doing her best to contain her attraction. With her pelvic floor tightening, she couldn't tell how long it'd be before her underwear became too damp to continue wearing.

Biceps, triceps, and pecs were thirsting to flex as a means of impression, but Nile discerned she wouldn't be swayed with a show. His smile was subtle as he raised his cup and nodded. Keeping his cool was necessary. He had already asked a question that she clearly thought was none of his business. And yet, she hadn't looked away from him. Her big, doe eyes locked onto his. He saw her mouth move but her words were inaudible. It was like she was telling herself something, perhaps a warning to stay away from him. Whatever it was, it thankfully hadn't warranted the breaking of their trance.

The outline of her hips hadn't lied. Those thighs were thick beneath her dress and Nile was already having visions of being on his knees, giving them their just praises. Her skin was fair and cheeks blooming red, no doubt from being stared at by a brawny police officer. *Look away for just two seconds, Nile. Let her know you're not a lurker.*

Finally, she did what he couldn't do for himself. Breaking the tension, she turned back to the counter. "Do you serve chocolate cake on any other days, or was I just lucking out deciding to come in on Thursdays? I mean, I don't drink coffee and your place is very calming. I'd like to do more to support."

Vashti, grinning uncontrollably, provoked Ms. Anada to join the conversation. "Joi here would like to know if we sell anything comparable to the Thursday Thrive during other days of the week. You think the Lime Crumble that Officer Nile orders would do her good?" At the mention of the officer's name, Vashti extended her arm in his direction.

Anada was tickled to have a chance to get in on the matchmaker play. Vashti was letting her in on the set up like she had tossed her an alley-oop. Anissa was also peering over, looking for collusion. She awaited Anada's response as if she didn't know the menu backwards and forward herself.

Noting their efforts, Anada replied, "No, that wouldn't do for her. Did you see the lines in her forehead scrunch at the mention of lime? Besides, I think she might need something a bit more decadent." Eyeing Nile, she hoped he'd known to step in at the insinuation.

Nile was desperate not to fumble this time. A whiff of Joi's perfume was sending bat signals to his loins. "The lime is my favorite but if you're searching for something with more cream, I'd suggest the Fudging Mondays Eclair roll," he offered with a onceover.

The watcher women all stood back. Anada clutched the heart pendant dangling from her neck. "Okay, Nile," she commended beneath her breath.

Presumably more noticeably than she intended, Joi gulped before engaging. "Is it chocolate through and through, though? Like all the way down to the center? Cause I love a good chocolate cream." Her soul was fixed on rearing its yearning head.

Licking his lips, Nile calculated his reply. If her inuendo was indeed intentional, she had to know, so was he. If he could nibble on her neck right then and watch her throw her head back in ecstasy while he massaged her ripe breasts, he would have. However, if what she was asking was innocent, he decided it wouldn't make the conversation any less provocative.

"All the way to the core. I promise it'll do right by you," he added confidently.

His pseudo cheerleading squad looked on from behind the counter. They grinned as they playfully nudged each other. Each breath was baited, wondering what would come next for the two moths trying to make sense of their flame. Thankfully, there were only a few straggling customers coming in and going out. Because Nile was all out of game. He needed the girls' presence to back him up. They, though, were so enthralled, they were motionless, looking on as a stadium of fans holding air, hoping for a touchdown. *No slick remarks to charm her information into my cell phone? Am I really that lame? Sheesh! I gotta work on some things.*

"Okay, then. I guess I'll be here on Monday to give it a try." Joi smiled. "Thank you for your help, Officer."

Wait, was that a wink? As she scurried to her car, Nile rushed out behind her. Slowing his pace, he watched her step into the driver's side of her ruby, late model Altima. He lowered his head for a clearer view. He aimed to ensure she hadn't been escorted to their destined rendezvous by a boyfriend or random overnight jock. *How would I even know the difference? Already she's got me out of my character.*

Her ring finger was bare, and he saw no tan line. *Technically, if she is with someone, he hasn't properly taken her off the market. If she were mine, there'd be no speculation.* Still, he wondered if she had been giving herself to someone else.

Anada came out to join him. She watched Joi drive off just as he did. "Did you give her your card, at least?" She handed him a paper bag with his favorite crumble inside. "Figured you might need this a little early today." She returned inside while Nile stood, bewildered.

TASTE OF sin

Sitting amongst the congregation at her mother and sister's preferred place of worship, *Come to The Temple: Women's Non-Denominational Church*, Joi bowed her head. "Dear Lord, it's me, Joi. Okay you probably already knew it was me, but you also know how much I struggle with my starts. Anyway, please help me to stop hating Caprice. I don't even want that demon of a man she's got, anymore. By the way, did you see that honey you sent me over at, Sweet Thangs? Of course, you've seen him. That was stupid. Anyway, Lord you are good and sovereign. So, with that in mind, release my ego and the feeling of embarrassment whenever Gordon comes to our place of business and the whole entire building knows he was mine first and now he's up Caprice's faux ass..."

She cupped her lips. *Why can't I keep it clean? I'm talking to God for goodness sake.* One eye closed, and the other wide as a Cyclops', she scoped her fellow congregants, hoping none could decipher the prayer she mouthed. A rich and colorful array of women in two-piece suits, with their heads hung and palms high gave no indication of being concerned with her. A good number of them had tears streaming down their faces as they murmured their requests, apologies, and dedications. Despite her prayer being what she intended to be an indecipherable whisper; her heart sunk with her inability to keep her little chat with God clear of foulness. To boot, her preference for an outfit that consisted of an apple red, off the shoulder, ribbed sweater and a pair of charcoal, pinstriped slacks made her stand out from the predominantly would-be Easter get-ups. She waved a hand over her bouncing, shoulder length, roller-set curls. *Now they probably think I'm vain, worrying about my hair. Why am I like this?*

"Girl, sit down and cut it out. Didn't nobody but me hear you," Camilla chastised. She tugged at her sister's trousers.

Reluctantly, Joi obliged. However, it was not without slowly stretching her neck, double checking who might have reserved judgement regarding her offensive language. Seeing as though the result was the same as the last time that she took inventory, she shook her head and sighed. *My own worst critic, just like Mama says.*

Camilla also shook her head, but then took to her own invocation. Clasping her hands, she prayed aloud. "Lord, please bring the girl some peace. She got anxiety about every doggone thing. Like you up there studying her cussing. It's just words we made up down here. And you know we light-skinned. Got her cheeks blooming like a rose bush. If anything, they gonna think she had a nasty thought before they think she said something profane. Truthfully, some of them could use the fantasy. Their attitudes just as dry, but I digress as that is not why I'm calling on you, good Lord. My sister is finer than baby hairs, intelligent, and made of pure sugar. That good for nothing, Gordon and his hot in the pants, extra messy of a plastic jellybean, concubine got her insecurities on high. Now she got her fingers all up in her hair, because I know she worried she ain't got a hat on. But neither do I. Ain't nobody got time for them big ole boats they up in here wearing. We're in this place to get your Word spoken to us. Child gonna miss all the gems Pastor Cleo spitting out today and now I'm going to have to spend my hard-earned money buying her the CD so she can listen on her own time. Her heart is clean, you know that Lord. Well, duh! You gave it to her. I just want the girl to get some sleep, so she not bat crazy. She already developed the hearing. 'Cause right now..." Camilla glanced over at her younger sibling.

Rolling her eyes at Camilla's longwinded request, Joi surveyed the room once more. As the intercession of the overheard prayer rewound in her mind, she questioned was Camilla truly the only one who heard her. *If I could just get out of my head for two seconds. But if you would send Mr. Chocolate Police Officer into my world once more, I'd know you forgave me for real and didn't take offense to my thoughts.*

Once again, Joi patted the top of her head, searching for unruly strands that needed to be smoothed. She could feel Camilla slink her arm around her shoulders. Joi knew to expect there to be a lecture on the way, and because they were in church, Camilla would take advantage of how difficult it would be for Joi to wiggle away without making a scene.

"Stop worrying about what everyone is thinking. There's no thought anyone could have about what you say or even your life, that's more important than what you think of yourself. So, try to think some empowering thoughts. Encourage yourself, like that song Mama used to sing before dropping us off at school every morning."

Try being the one everyone knows as half-crazy because her so-called boyfriend screwed another woman in their bed. Joi nodded. The burning in her pupils warned of an impending flood. Holding onto the stick fan issued by the usher, Joi fanned herself, hoping the slight breeze would keep the budding emotions at bay.

Marjorie Briar usually sat between her daughters in the pews, but the arthritis in her knees had been acting up and she wasn't up to walking. Over the years as her condition developed, on Sundays where she couldn't make it, she would find comfort in her favorite tune to hum. As of late, it seemed she hummed more frequently when Joi came around. She'd touch her hand, motion for Joi to get closer, plant a kiss to her forehead, then remind her youngest child that trouble wouldn't last always.

Katoi, who was sitting on the opposite side of Camilla, had kept quiet as expected of her. But with the constant whispering chatter, she was urged to insert herself in whatever soothing her beloved Aunt required. She reached across her mother. "I want to hug on Aunt Joi, too. Can I, Mom?" Her Bambi eyes looked into the freckled face of her mother, pleading the question.

Camilla fluffed her daughter's rusty red afro puffs. Unable to resist the sincerity in which her youngest daughter loved on her baby sister, Camilla shifted her weight, angling her knees to give way. Affectionately, she watched, considering the child's excitement to be granted the right to rise from her seat and walk down the pew to the person she idolized. Years of being ordered to sit still while in the sanctuary, cautioned this would be a seldom exception.

I swear Milla has my baby girl whipped into shape like how Mama had us. But good God, let her not spring loose the way Milla and I did once High School became a thing.

"Come here, Kitty. You know Auntie loves your hugs." Joi welcomed her with outstretched arms.

The young girl's caramel cuteness yearned for pinches and kisses. Her aunt grinned to as she eyed her navy-blue overall dress with big white buttons and matching white turtleneck. *Camilla and her style. Kitty will own a fashion line complete with runway models when it's all said and done, if Milly has any say so.* Joi shook her head.

Katoi's contentment was raised to the next level, when she was pulled onto Joi's lap. For the past two years, the eight-year-old had been told she was too big or too heavy for such an endearment, but today, on Sunday morning, love was the only rule that wouldn't be broken. It was a good thing too, because there was something she had to get off of her chest.

"Auntie?" Katoi spoke softly, careful not to warrant being plucked for speaking while the Pastor was giving her sermon.

Joi peeked over at Camilla who had shifted to being completely engrossed. "Yes, baby?"

"I had a dream about you last night. There was a whole bunch of love hearts in the air and in it, you were happy. Your smile was pretty like when we open gifts on Christmas morning."

Wow! Can I only be happy in a child's dream? The mere fact that her niece needed to mention such a dream caused Joi's heart to pick up pace. "Awe Kitty, I'm always happy when I'm with you." Though she knew the girl was revealing she could see much deeper than the exterior Joi thought she was portraying, she tried to reassure her anyway.

"But I'm not finished. There were fluttering butterflies, all different colors like a rainbow, and they were making a circle around you wherever you went. But all you ate for every meal was chocolate cake." Tickled by the memory, Kitty's mood brightened.

Salivating over the wish for another taste of her Thursday pleasure, Joi reminded herself to keep focus on Kitty's dream. "Well, I do love chocolate cake. But for every meal? What did I drink?"

The child shrugged her shoulders. "I don't know. Maybe some coffee?"

The two of them bellied over with muffled laughter. Although, Joi had her reservations. *Weird dream. And why would she say coffee? I don't even drink the stuff. Off the wall.*

Shushed by one of the gloved ushers, they closed their mouths, doing their best to swallow the pending howls, but continued being amused, nonetheless. Butterflies and chocolate cake made for quite a fantastical picture, but the coffee is what was still sitting with Joi, really. Despite never being a coffee drinker, she did get her weekly delicacy from a bakery that very much mirrored a coffee shop. And the magnificent view of an officer with his thick arms and succulent lips held a cup of expresso while she asked God to one day let her be the morning force he'd hold in his hands. However, this was something Katoi couldn't have been privy to. Camilla would have no need to confide any information about Sweet Thangs, as much as she reminded the child to keep out of grown folks' business. Besides finding out about her run in with Mr. Too Fine, the shop was just some place her little sister frequented on Thursdays.

Wouldn't it be a beautiful world if Kitty was somehow having a premonition? I'd love to be full of flutters, and I'm sure I would be if he was the chocolate to my cake. He seemed so strong, seriously sexy, and the way he stood with his legs gapped, I know he's probably working with something that could put a hurting on me. Oh crap, we're still in church. I'm sorry, Lord. I should just go. I'm obviously not paying attention to what's being preached. Just can't seem to keep my mind out of a New York City sewer, today.

Joi lifted Kitty from her lap and then lowered her beside her. Although, she noticed the girl appeared disturbed. Normally, she hated to see Joi prepare to go, which, by the way, she could always sense a good thirty minutes beforehand, but this felt different. This twist of the lips, folded arms, and furrowing of brow was like Joi had suddenly cut her off. As if they were having an in-depth conversation in which Joi was exiting mid-sentence.

But I can't stay. My mind is all over the place and if Mama were here, she'd read my fidgets and know the thoughts I've had in here. She would whip my grown tail to the white meat.

Just as Joi was reaching for her heather gray maxi coat, which was straddled across the back of the pew, Katoi, who was using her foot to rub out a blemish on the cream tile, had one more thing to say. "My mom says you think a lot about what you might consider mistakes, and that's what makes you sad." At the tail end of her sentence, she turned her head to meet her aunt's expression. There was a wealth of worry behind her young golden soul searchers.

Joi sighed. *This poor baby is stressed over my heart. Goodness, God, maybe this is the preaching I'm supposed to listen to. I got you.*

Pulling Katoi back over, Joi enveloped her into her bosom. "Your mom tells you too much. You're too young to get your mind mulling over such things."

Recalling her consideration for going into the bake shop again tomorrow, Joi was determined to shoo the rising fear away. *Truthfully, the éclair is of no interest to me. He is, though. Something about the way that enticing, hulk of a man wore his badge, did create some type of shift within me. I kind of want to see how real it is. He seemed honorable, not conceited like Gordon, and if I'm not totally out of my mind, he was interested, in me. Maybe he would help me get to better tomorrows. Or maybe I could help myself. Either way, Kitty needs me to promise to try to live up to my name.*

She nestled her nose into her niece's neck. What she was about to say would need to be heard clearly. "Katoi Hamilton, I promise that I will stop overthinking and let myself live. I will work to remove my victim mindset and try to latch on to some of that energy and love you, your mom, and even your dad, so effortlessly exude."

Katoi, smiled. "I remember that word from the spelling bee." Looking up into Joi's genuine eyes, she held up her pinky. "Do you pinky swear?"

Obliging her need for confirmation of the promise, Joi intertwined her fifth finger with Kitty's. It was possible she needed the boundless examination of a pondering child to reveal her somber mood wasn't hers alone, but one she was gifting to those who loved her.

I mean I let Gordon and Caprice make me hate Thursdays. A whole freaking day on the calendar that comes around every week. Uncle Bruce would say that's an awful lot of power I'm giving up. Well, in my defense, it did lead me to the best chocolate cake I've ever tasted in life. Although, I'm sure it has a heap of calories that are sure to show up on my hips in a minute. Still, I think I will go to Anada's tomorrow. Maybe I'll get a batch of those Mini Mixed-Berry Muffins for the office. Surprise everyone with an upbeat smile to match. They'll probably call security. Joi's pulse quickened as she dreamt of the possibilities. Clapping her hands, she stood and joined in the choir's exuberant chant, "I have new life…"

FUDGING Mondays

Nile peeked his head into his favorite, sweet café. For a Monday, the forty or so customers seemed pretty controlled. They received their orders and filed out, darting to their destinations. There were fewer school children than on Thursdays, but that didn't stop the overhead speakers from boasting its 90's Hip Hop serenade. Although there was the rapid buzz of paying customers, there was a different energy when there weren't the cliques of youth chiming along with the lyrics as though they were released during their time.

No matter. As long as she shows. He inspected the shop, searching for who or what wasn't even a date. She made no promises despite how hard he tried to sell her on the éclair, but he was inclined to believe she'd fulfill his anticipation. If she wasn't attracted to him the way he was drawn to her, it would leave him confused and thoroughly discouraged.

Vashti elbowed Anissa. "She's here," she whispered.

Noticing the bouncing curls, which could hardly be tamed by the beaming red applejack hat, Nile swung around to see Joi looking like sunshine beneath a black wool, leather trimmed, trench coat. The hat slightly tilted, gave way to those big brown eyes. Her lips, a darker shade of rouge, inspired his imagination to run through scenarios of his fingers inside them, sharing the taste of her juices. Then picturing her laying on his back while she kissed the, "God Is My Witness," tattoo across his blades had him yearning to flip her on her back and hear those lips speak his name while he tongued his hopes into her lower set.

"Joi! You came back. To try the éclair?" Anada bustled from behind the counter. She stretched her arm to take Joi over to the encased array of Monday specialties.

"I think I'll forgo the chocolate goodness of that roll today, Ms. Anada. Sorry. I know I told you I was coming in for your famed sweetness, but if I start, I may not be able to stop. May I have some tea instead? That peppermint smells like Christmas morning. But please hold the expresso."

Looking up from handing out the plethora of ordered Donut Fudge Tips, Anissa smiled broadly. She leaned in. Casually, Nile strolled over to hear what secret she was anxious to share.

"Should I ask her for her number for you? 'Cause in a minute your only option is going to be to get Vashti to give it to you, and you know she's going to give you the hardest time about it. Step up to the plate, big man."

Receiving her warning, Nile straightened his back. *Yeah, I need to go hard or go and be alone at home.* Joi was still deciding if she'd try something from what Anada was offering as a free sample menu. He was in her peripheral though. He could feel it.

Just as Joi was being handed her honey laced Mintspresso Tinsel Tea, minus the wakeup shot, Nile stood beside her. "I don't believe I asked you directly for your name the other day. I'd completely make a fool of myself as a man if I made the same mistake twice." He fixated on her eyes, hoping she'd be tempted to fall into his. *Let's hope this works and she doesn't call me out on my bull, because I absolutely know her name.*

Joi sipped her tea. From the way she flinched he assumed it was as hot as dripping lava. Anada's tea always needed a good few minutes to cool. Nile could tell she was forcing herself to stay calm and recover quickly. Instead of being completely distracted by the sting, she smiled.

"Joi. I'd shake your hand, but you know, hot tea. Could never hold a hot cup with just one hand."

"Yes, Joi. We should get our footing right from beginning, so I will come clean. I did hear Anada refer to your name the other day. I just didn't want to use it without your permission. Joi, though, seems to be a fitting name for a woman like you."

At the sound of her name spilling from his lips, her heart began pounding its war cry. Her breath became caught between the back of her tongue and the plunge of her breast. She looked him over. Her smile was bright. *Say something else. Anything but please add my name to it you sexy mother fuc...*

The few remaining consumers had passed through. For the two gravitating crushers the world held less weight. He, her, with the grinning bunch looking on, fading into the background.

"Sorry, I'm really not trying to game you. I think I just wanted to hear you say it. In case, you know, you weren't interested in giving it out. It's corny but you've certainly added joy to my day."

She nodded. Shyly, Joi surveyed the room. "My mother would be happy to hear you say that. She named me." She chuckled. It seemed as though she got lost in her mind for a second. But then she added, "My sister would appreciate it for different reasons."

Before he read too much into her exhale, Nile decided he needed to just go for it. "My apologies if this is out of order, but you're breathtaking."

Her cheeks flushed and eyes glossed. He hoped he hadn't said anything to send her into flight. "I'm sorry if you think I'm being inappropriate." *What if my breath stinks? It smells like coffee. What if she doesn't like coffee. Maybe she can pick up on the caramel. Who doesn't like the smell of caramel? Is this my first time? What the hell?*

"No, no, I'm sorry. I just had a bunch of thoughts run through my mind. It happens a lot. But no, you're fine." She bit her lip. "And I mean that in every sense," she flirted.

As if she knew Vashti and Anissa were standing behind her, one with a pen and the other with a napkin, she reached up. Leaving Anada to tend to the few patrons alone, the two young women were more than happy to hand Joi the supplies. She jotted her number. He watched in awe of her radiance until he realized he was putting her in a position to take the lead. It was okay if that's how she preferred to do things, but unlike his ordeal with Liana, he needed her to know she was wanted, and as his father would surmise, "chased after."

Handing her his card in exchange for the napkin full of scribbles, he pointed out, "The number on the back is my cell. I want you to recognize it when you see it, so you'll answer my call." He winked. "Don't have me out here calling and you declining me like a scammer. And you should expect me today. I'm going to call you, today." Nile smirked. *Whew! That boy recovery game is bad!*

"Are you sure?" She glanced down at his card. "Mr. Nile Ledger." His name rolled around her tongue like melted ice cream. "Don't make a promise you can't keep. I'd understand if it took a while. These streets probably keep you pretty busy, especially if you're patrolling around here." Tongue in cheek, she tapped the card against her palm.

From the kitchen, Anada came bursting through the swinging door, carrying a hot tray of her cocoa croissants. "What are you two young ladies standing around for? My goodness, if I thought I'd be working alone, I would've known to save myself some money. Could've just given you the day off, since you seem to be taking it anyway." She placed the tray in the open space cleared specially to receive its goods. Upon siting Joi and Nile's locked stare she paused. "Oh, I see."

Choosing not to break the trance the beautiful specimen held him in, Nile confirmed his interest. "There is nothing that would keep me from the opportunity to get to know you. I'm much too grateful for that."

Her face glistened like nighttime stars, right there in the middle of the morning. "Good. So, I don't need to gain the week load of extra calories I've been tempted to, while I waited to see if you'd do anything more than just eyeball me," she chortled.

Looking away was nearing impossible for Nile. He was attempting to pierce her thoughts. Understand who she was and why she would let herself be fooled into thinking it would be so easy to mess with her perfection. *Who was it that had her feeling so flawed? She could eat whatever she wanted, and it wouldn't add or subtract from the exclamation of perfection illuminating from her being. If she'd let me, I'd do whatever she'd need me to do in order to love all her doubts away. Listen to me. She got me all poetic and what not.*

Their moment of time-stoppage was interrupted by the screeching charade of a seemingly out-of-place greeting. "Oh my God, Joi! Haven't seen you in like a trillion years. Did you switch departments? I heard that you might've. Congrats on the new job, I guess. What a small world. I had no idea you came here too. Isn't this place incredible? I was just telling bae he had to come in and try the Cup of Crumbs Cheesecake."

Bliss on hold, Joi's smile dissipated. Daggering a glance at the young woman, an unbelievable imitation of tolerance sleeked across her lips. "Well Caprice, you do like crumbs."

Caprice's lips parted but no sound emerged. Her off season tanned cheeks reddened. "You right. But listen, did they turn your water off this morning too? I heard half the neighborhood was out due to Municipal flushing the hydrants. Girl, I'm so glad I'm an early riser. Both Gordon and I were able to take showers in the nick of time. You good, though?" Her lips pursed as she intentionally travelled her eyes up and down Joi's frame.

A blush for a blush. Joi's embarrassment colored her entire face. Both Anissa and Vashti stood behind the pastry display, glowering at the loud talking, discernibly envious, converser. Anissa too through with the barging woman's energy, stormed over to the register.

"Cup of Crumbs," Vashti announced as she pounded the plastic cup onto the counter. "Please pay the cashier." She nodded in Anissa's direction.

Scrutinizing Vashti's face it seemed a lightbulb went off. "Figures." Backing down from what appeared to be morphing into a full-on standoff with Joi equipped with back-up in tow, Caprice accepted her treat. She hadn't even noticed Vashti balling her fists at her sides. With a huff and a swerve of her head, Caprice obliged, handing Anissa a five-dollar bill. "Tell Ms. Anada I said, keep the change. I love what she's doing here. Such great charity." Then just as she entered, she slithered out.

Releasing the breath she had boxed up in her chest, Joi began to follow suit. Making it out into the parking lot, her steps livened. She had become unnerved.

Dissatisfied with the turn of events, Nile hastened behind her. There was no way he would let her go without seeing to her mental. *I know she's not about to let that fake, I don't even know what to call her, ruin her day. Dammit, why didn't I interrupt? Just stood there and watched her discomfort. Nice going, leaving her unprotected.*

Reaching the door of her sedan, Joi felt around in her pocket for her car keys. Gripping the Nissan clicker, she eagerly yanked on the door handle. Once Nile caught up to her, she was ready to shut her door, but he tugged at her elbow.

"On my off days I help train the neighborhood athletes at the Community Center. If ever they have running water and you don't, just know we have a women's locker room I can get you access to."

Joi rubbed a hand over her forehead. "You're sweet and now I'm embarrassed, so I think I should go."

He eyed her clearly manicured hands as they gripped the steering wheel. His pulse was throwing boulders against his skin. Despite his heart racing, he managed to remind himself to be intentional. "Don't forget, my personal number is on the back too. You know, in case you need anything else. Like dinner. Or maybe some chocolate cake."

Slowly tasting his lips, he kept his attention on her face. If anything was going to leave her flustered, it was going to be how strong he was coming on. Not some wench trying to get under her skin. *Definitely taking this one for the team.*

Her joy creeping back into her cheeks, she blessed him with another wink. A few more minutes of her time and he had fallen for her for real. *Her spirit feels easy, not complicated and manipulative. Yet like most women, she has probably withstood a multitude of storms.* She was as precious and complicated as the earth. If given the chance he'd wash her over like the ocean.

"Seek and find," he reminded himself, barely above a whisper. The message from the Sunday morning evangelist that visited his parents' house this past week reverberated throughout his consciousness. "Whatever you need, Ms. Joi, I'd relocate heaven to get you there. That is, if you answer my call."

SUGAR*less*

Sitting at her desk, Joi felt like she had made it to home base. *Had I known I was going to run into Caprice, I would've gotten the éclair.* Her tea was still warm, but not nearly as comforting as a piece of chocolate would be. As she took a sip, she sighed, recalling the trajectory of her morning.

At forty-four minutes after four, there wasn't any sunlight. Still, Joi was awake, awaiting her presumed cafe date. The night before she had drifted off at nine o'clock and it was only now that she was opening her eyes.

"Best sleep I've had in months," she said aloud into the empty bedroom. *"But now I've got all this silly schoolgirl angst."*

Like a techno baseline, her heart was pulsating. She swung her legs over the side of the bed, per usual, although this rising was welcomed and didn't incite a grunt. Taking her time through her routine, she smiled at each interval of accomplishment. Flossing was almost enjoyable. Brushing her teeth was as meticulous as putting on a full face of makeup. Adding a bit of whitener, she inspected her chompers in the mirror.

"Would you look at that? I can actually take care of myself when

I'm not pressed for time or when I'm not brooding half the morning. Maybe I'll even go for a bubble bath."

Thinking about luxuriating in the garden tub with bubbles up to her chin, Joi recalled the previous incident when she had allowed herself to do such a thing. "Camilla would have my head if I fell back asleep and blamed it on a pamper soak. No matter how much she encourages them damn pleasure baths." She amused herself. The anticipation for the day ahead was nothing she could compare to feeling in the past.

"I can just imagine her calling my phone ten thousand times, filling up my voicemail." Joi had a hearty laugh. "A shower it is. But I can make it full of steam like at the spa Mama took me to for my birthday."

She sauntered the few feet to the glass-cased shower. Yanking open the door; she slid her arm in and began turning the knob. No drip.

"Wait. What's happening?" She turned the other. Still nothing. "Are you freaking kidding me?"

Refusing to believe all hope for water had been stripped from her morning so suddenly, Joi quickened back over to the tub. The faucet hissed then sung but held out on its release. She ran back to the sink where she had carried on a full facewash, and her dental maintenance without a problem. A couple residue drops leaked, but the stream had taken leave.

"Well if this ain't the devil." Joi stomped her way into the bedroom to look at the calendar she kept hung on the back of the bedroom door.

Each day she took off from work, there was a red circle around it. Flipping through the pages, she counted. "Crap, I only have one day left. All that stupid ass time I took off sulking over Gordon and Caprice, and now I can't even call off to figure out how I'm going to wash my ass. The one day I decide to move on, and the Universe has got my foot caught in a mouse trap. Ugh!"

After shouting to the heavens, then shoving her face into an oversized pillow, compelled to take a bite and rip it to shreds like a mad dog, Joi sat up on the bed and picked up her cell phone. It was twenty minutes before six. "And how the hell did it take me a whole damn hour to get up and do absolutely nothing but wash my face?" She plopped back and dialed her sister's number.

Groggily, Camilla answered. "Everything okay?"

"Water's out. Just as I'm calling, I can vaguely recall a flyer posted on the door downstairs. Must be flushing it or testing it or something. Of all the days." She pulled her legs in beneath her and crossed them.

"Sounds about right for a Monday. But what do you have going on today that makes this especially catastrophic?" Camilla hummed a familiar tune of comfort.

Joi became suspicious. She could picture Camilla with her eyes closed. It was odd that she was not only more alert at this time in the morning, but without the background rumble of Katoi being rushed out of the bathroom or demanding breakfast. Something was afoot.

"Milla? You better not be getting nasty while you're on the phone with me." Joi jumped from crossed legs, onto the floor and into a warrior combat stance. "I can't take a shower. This is an actual crisis! And Terrence probably over there feeling on your booty like your hiding a genie in there and y'all seventeen. Where's Kitty?"

"First of all..." It never took Camilla long to reclaim her sass.

Joi was willing to bet fifty dollars the siren had her eyebrows furrowed, gliding her tongue over her gums, deciding what venom she'd spew to get her younger sibling back in check. Her energy levels were increasing. Breath being forced though her pursed lips, Joi knew she could only be sitting upright.

"Don't be mad at me, cause your booty only get rubbed by the seat of the toilet. Second of all, my child is with Nani, our Mama, if you must know. She said she missed her, so I dropped Kitty off last night. Uncle Bruce is taking her to school this week. Excuse me for taking a day off to lay up with my husband. It's your old funky attitude that really needs cleaning, I tell you that. But anyway, did you have sex with yourself last night?"

Mouth agape, Joi stumbled to find the words to reply. "I, uh, what? What does this have to... No, but you're really going to ask me that in front of Terrence?"

Surveying her bedroom, and the complete disarray she had left it in the night before, she began to pick up her tossed clothes from the floor. She could hear her mother's nagging voice in her head, prompting her to take better care of her possessions or lose them. Joi mumbled with rolled eyes, "Gordon was a thing, but never mind."

"Oh honey, hush. You think I'm trying to give my boo visions of your self-pleasing? He ran downstairs for a glass of water. So, before he comes back up hydrated and demanding my time, which I'm most definitely about to give him, answer me. Would it make you feel any better if I threw in the possibility of you having it with someone else?" Camilla scoffed.

"Oh-em-gee, no. None of that. I had a peaceful rest. Like really good. Even woke up in a mood I hadn't felt in forever. Actually, I felt optimistic. I was looking forward to the Sugar Rush, and now I've got to go through the day smelling like deodorant atop of overnight funk, skin, and lotion," Joi whined.

"A good mood, huh? That Sugar Rush adding more sugar to your morning on a Monday now? You better not drown yourself in dead weight and diabetes over this dude." At the same time, she was placing her first stick of gum for the day, in her mouth.

"How is it possible I can hear your finger wagging? And the fact you're popping gum in my ear like you're actually aiming to chew a hole in your teeth don't make you any better."

Succumbing to the idea that work was a must, Joi followed the short hallway into what was supposed to be her spare bedroom. Boasting a plush midnight futon, which she picked up for fifty dollars at a garage sale, the room was somewhat of an extensive closet. As a gift to herself after the break-up, she designed it as her way to peace. She'd look in the full-length mirror and force her consciousness to admire the woman that stood before it. Shoe racks lined the soft pink walls. A fuzzy champagne colored rug adorned the center of the wood planks. White Christmas lights bordered the walls' creases and gold picture frames hung in arrangements throughout. "One day I'm going to fill you with pictures of love and a happy life, I promise," she whispered, nearly forgetting Camilla was still on the other end of the phone.

"You're a damn bat," Milla snapped.

As kids, Camilla hated her little sister's supreme hearing. Joi would overhear her plans to skip school with Terrence. She'd have to pay her a whole dollar to keep her from spilling the beans to their Mama.

"So, what's really up? Did you finally find a sight to set on? Is that what, or should I say is that who has you melting down on today? Can't get your scent, right?" Charmed by her own wit, Camilla howled.

"You're annoying." Joi couldn't help her grin. The image of the chocolate, uniformed, stoic blessing with deep-set eyes came flashing through her mind. His arms she concluded, were strong enough to lift her in the air and boy, did she want to get lifted.

Taking heed to her caller's moment of silence, Camilla wasted no time giving herself what she believed was an appropriate kudo. "You can't even protest with confidence. I told you once you open your eyes to the world, you'll finally see all that's in it for you. Anyway, if you wasn't doing any fornicating, then you should be good. Some folks don't even bathe on a daily. Did you see that post about people not washing their legs? It was like on every social media site. You know that's that bull. Anyway, if I know you, there was a long ass shower last night. It's obvious you ain't never had a house full of folks driving your damn bill up to the heavens. I've been your sister your whole life. The only time you smelled of horrible hygiene was the one year you thought you were training to try out for the basketball team. You remember that? Once you found out you'd be the shortest person on the team and would be expected to play point guard, you quit with a middle finger and had the nerve to offer an apology, even though it was being tossed over your shoulder."

Admittedly, Camilla's cackling delighted Joi. Every time she thought the earth was about to split open and swallow her whole, her lifelong best friend would pull her out and shed some light. "How you turn my worries into tears of laughter each and every time, I have no idea."

"I was never prouder than that day. And my nostrils had never again rejoiced as much as they did. Mama went to the alter and thanked the Lord."

Rummaging through her closet, Joi felt renewed and ready to meet that tantalizing expression and those full lips. She settled on a maroon colored cotton skirt and mouthed to herself, "This one clings to my hips nicely. In case I need to sway. Maybe I can stop in and let him watch me from afar." Although, going to meet a man with less than freshly bathed underarms was not high on her list of Must Tries, Camilla's confidence had been transferred and absorbed.

Camilla sighed then, cleared her throat. "Terrence is back. Before I go, I want to tell you this one thing."

"And here we go with the sappiness. I know you love me. There is nothing to be afraid of long as I have that knowledge. People are not puppets. Patterns may be indicators, but the beauty of humans is when they join in with the Universe they were created in. I should live and love without bounds. Blah, blah, blah. Let the chips fall where they may. Trusting in my own ability to recover will bless my heart, time and time again." Joi cheesed. Reciting Camilla's repetitious speech did make her feel better, although she'd never let on to her sister's credit.

"It seems my job is done then. Go meet a guy. Eat your cake. Then call Mama when you're done. 'Cause I'm offline for the remainder of the day. Goodbye my pretty."

The playfully sinister laugh was all Joi could hear as her motivator had apparently pressed the end icon on her phone. Gliding her stocking up each leg, Joi took a deep breath. "What's mine is mine. Besides, who cares about the opinion of a stranger?"

Now back in her office, as she finished her tea, Joi felt a sense of calm. The pace of her bouncing blood vessels had slowed.

Caprice tried me, for sure. But Mr. Nile Ledger just might be designed for me.

And she did care about his opinion.

But he sure as hell didn't care about ole girl's. Not once did he take his eyes off of me. He wasn't the least bit swayed by her shade, or my underarms.

Remnants of their interaction still paced through her mind.

His baritone snuck up on her.

My goodness his voice is the kind that leaves you cold sweating at night after a two-minute conversation.

It careened through her eardrums, teasing her nipples. Afraid to turn around, look into his eyes, and give over to compulsion, she wondered what it was she would say.

That was crazy. All that worry and ain't even think about conversation.

After all Camilla had juiced her with, she still hadn't planned for talking to him.

A true testament to my awkwardness.

Swallowing her instinct to whip around and press her lips onto his, she counted to three before replying to any of his questions.

He probably thought I was out of my mind, talking to myself.

Mentally, she pleaded with him not to come any closer. Her body temperature was already rising. The last thing she needed was to excrete her nerves and run him away with what she could only imagine to be a sweaty stench.

Not when I could picture the future with his face poised and placed among photos on my wall. Hell, I've got a spot right here for him on my desk.

Recalling the numerous times she had heard her brother-in-law tell her to be easy, she charged herself to let whatever was going to happen, take place. There was too much of her validation riding on what this strange man, whom she'd only met once, would think of her.

At least I convinced myself.

So, she flirted; let him invade her space.

Then here comes Caprice. Had to blow me up, talking about some doggone water. Vashti definitely had my back, though.

Vashti had dealt with Caprice at the Admissions office when she was refuting being placed into a Speech class. She'd come to Joi's office complaining the girl was as fake and as petty as she was proving to be there in the cafe.

I don't know why I aborted mission. Couldn't even look him in the eye. Retreated to my damn car. Now that felt like a fail. I was so afraid that he'd think I was some broken down damsel, whose almost out on the streets and just needs somewhere to wash. What a time to forget to unpack the two boxes of shoes I have propped up on the backseat.

It was hard to deny her fear at the time. She convinced herself that if she continued to stand around, she would've been late, and more feelings of failure was out of the question. She was tapped out for the day. Cradling her knees on the living room floor, listening to vintage Mary J. Blige love songs, was a scene her somber heart was working to lure her into creating.

But no Sir, my man wouldn't let up. A true gentleman, assuring I was okay. Dinner sounded nice and chocolate cake of course sounded splendid.

It would be that very truth that had her replaying the entire exchange, fantasizing about his fingers running through her curls.

Or his arms nestled around my shoulders as we slept.

Joi's heart was hammering through her chest. Blood on fire, her cheeks were glowing like a fluorescent lamp. *Is he asking me out?* She asked herself the question again, hesitant to believe she had really reached the light at the end of her tunnel. Mondays were morphing into her most looked forward to day of the week.

It was taking all of my strength not to close my eyes and, thank God at the exact moment in which he called me, "breathtaking."

However, she did make a mental note to praise dance once she got to work. A promise she was about to make good on.

Camilla is going to lose her wig when I tell her this one.

JUST A *sample*

Evening brought about the quiet of the pending night. Cars cruised the rainy roads after long days and Nile's QX80 was in that number. Although he had planned to call Joi immediately after his shift, booking three members of an underaged gang ran him well over the hours when the sun was shining.

"Hello?" He likened her voice to the pleasure of a dripping strawberry on a summer day.

Turning the volume of the car speaker up a notch, it occurred to him that he hadn't planned his speech. "Hey. It's Nile. The guy you met..."

Her chuckle was glittered with effortless truth. "I know who you are. I've been waiting for you to call me. How are you? How was your day?"

"Eventful." He wished he could tell her of all his anxieties. How he yearned to find a way to cease the community's gang activity. Hopes were for a quiet Christmas were dismantling. The day still rewinding and flashing before his eyes, he wheeled the SUV into the lot of his development.

All throughout the day, the rain made for a slickness that had the entire city driving as if they were walking on ice. It wasn't anyone's fault, though, that Nile was anxious to get home. As much as he could, he avoided honking his horn and cursing the creeping drivers. If there was one night he wanted to speed, it was tonight. Finally, at the finish line, his mind was still clouded. *"Calling all units to Grade D. Shots fired, I repeat shots fired! On the one hundred-block of Rosehill. Calling all units."* Sheryl's dispatch still rang in his hearing.

"One-word answers, huh? Sounds pretty loaded."

Nile was losing the battle to not get too lost in his head. *"They want to kill each other, then we should let them. Out here being savages and we've got to play zookeeper."* Fellow officer, Daniel Gregory's words were like ignited kerosene. Cocky, he was without regard to him being a five-foot-seven, stick thin, hook nose. He spit a wad of tobacco, while theorizing the situation. In Grade D, everyone to him was a gangster, drug-dealer, a prostitute, or low life, but always unworthy of anyone's time.

"Loaded is appropriate. Sometimes it's hard to shake the day loose," Nile admitted as he wedged his key in the door of his townhome. Choosing to keep the lighting dim, he removed his standard issued footwear and placed his wet overcoat on the doorknob of the coat closet.

Today, it took us three hours to get the three teens to stand down. Each taking possession of a firearm that could've taken out the ten-man squad we had on the premises. Tensions were high but throwing our hands up and letting these kids put holes in each other wasn't going to happen if I could help it. But nearly coming to blows with Gregory for his twisted, privileged, white-washed point of view wasn't the answer either.

Everything was on the tip of his tongue, but this was his first real conversation with the beauty. Dumping his worries at her feet, he determined was not the impression he was looking to make. He swallowed.

"Alright, well lay it on me," Joi directed as if he had some piece of news, she expected him to share.

Afternoons were slow at Sweet Thangs. It was a guilty pleasure to go sit with the crew and pass the time. It was something Nile knew he'd no longer be able to do once the department issued him a new partner. It had taken much longer than expected. But he assumed, that was just the script. Until, earlier that morning he had been informed Officer Gregory was now assigned as his partner.

Once the last of the late morning rush trotted in and out about fifteen minutes to ten, there were seldom any customers at the bake shop. Anada never complained though. The hush gave her the opportunity to think up new recipe ideas, using the girls as taste testers. What she dubbed, "the fun part," she looked forward to everyday. By the time Nile had joined them, they'd be settled on what they'd add to the menu, using his taste buds as confirmation.

With no children of her own, it was time, Anada concluded, for her to pass her knowledge to Anissa. She knew the girl adored her and if she would one day slow down and hand over the reins to her shop, the young apprentice would make the optimal choice. Vashti, on the other hand, although having no interest in inheriting what would soon be a legacy, had quick wit and her daily commentary on the morning's events kept the energy flowing. Best of all, she was genuine in her evaluations of Anada's experimental creations. Her tongue could detect a pinch of too much salt, a slight spillage of sugar, or a need for cinnamon. Today's highlight was, Vanilla Cranberry Cookies. Nile considered himself lucky to be able to grab one before the incoming dispatcher's call. Once the alert came in, a different kind of energy stormed the gathering.

Jumping in the squad car, Nile sped down the streets, hoping not to see another body bag. Two weeks had gone by without a casualty. It was a streak for the neighborhood, and he was naïve enough to think it meant they were on the road to healing. The three rival gangs normally occupying the section of the community had no remorse. Once officers uniformly marched in, they'd draw their weapons, routinely making the news for standoffs. An afternoon call, just as today, habitually lasted into the night. They wore death like a badge of honor. Although Nile and his unit were lucky to have come out of tonight's fiasco without casualties, it wasn't without hours of persuasion. There were some on the squad who would prefer to put a bullet in each of the perpetrators, but all he saw was additional murders. More sons on the ground. More bloodshed and more discord.

Trekking upstairs to his bedroom, Nile thought about his pending response. *We can't start like this. Our talks should be full of questions about her favorite color, why she glowed at the mention of Christmas morning, her favorite musicians, and what kinds of food she likes. Not about my daily struggles, disappointments, and my so-called mission with joining the department not panning out in the idealistic way I had hoped.* She was the reason he hadn't gone to get his work-out in. He couldn't waste another moment thinking about her without getting to know if she'd maybe been thinking about him too.

"Nah we good. Tell me about your day."

Replaying her infectious smile and her candor when referencing her embarrassment had his insides jumping at the chance to hear her talk, about anything. Changing out of his work attire and into a pair of dark gray sweats, he listened to her breathing. It was steady for a second, picked up pace and then it settled again. Like she was reassuring herself of some newly found fact. *Who are you, Miss Joi? Tell me what makes your heart break, so I can never come close.*

"I rather not. You're not the only one having trouble shaking the day loose." Her tone was doubtful. Silence followed.

Something had her desperately trying to avoid talking about how her day played out and it was suddenly of more concern to him than how his went. A swarm of emotions sat on Nile's chest. Guilt for not allowing her to escape into his details. Anger against whomever would've caused her day to be anything but as bright as her aura. *I hope it's not still that broad from this morning. I'm not even really sure what really went down. It just felt strange.* Then, yearning, for her to be next to him. She sounded like she could use the warmth of someone holding her, easing her spirit. He was trying to be that someone.

Bare chested and jogging back down the stairs, Nile forgot about his daily anticipation for turning on the night's basketball game. Joi would require all of his attention. "Whose got your light dimming, Beautiful? You can confide in me. I promise, no judgement." Once again, the woman at Sweet Thangs came to mind. She seemed to be adamant about speaking to Joi. Although Joi was apparently unwelcoming to whatever it was, she thought she offered. "It was kind of obvious you weren't feeling whomever that woman was this morning."

Sighing, Joi proceeded to tell Nile about who the woman was, Caprice. Her words were rapid. One skipped behind the other, yet she maintained her spirited personality. "We were living together, and then he cheated with her, and now he's dating her. And she just won't freaking graduate."

Nile hadn't expected her to go into such detail about her past relationship. However, he appreciated the glimpse into what made her tick and get ticked off. Disgusted at the display of self-centered and tactless treatment of whom he was now inwardly referring to as his Joi, he bit his tongue. When he was coming up, he would have his own choice words for what to call a woman picking on one he cared about. But as a man, he did as his father taught and minimized the disrespect. No matter how much it seemed warranted.

However, what followed had the means to stir his jealousy. Joi rattled on telling of the surprise visit she received from her ex on the tails of her finishing up her tea. His gall was most shocking to her. He aimed to annoy her, she supposed as she promised herself to remain professional in her work setting.

"I swear he only dropped by because Caprice saw me talking to you. She probably thought she was telling him something in passing and he saw it as a way to try to terrorize me. 'Thought I'd let you know how good you looked today.' Had I not cared so much about my boots, I would've taken one off and bunted it at his head. There was no reason for him to even be in the building. He's never been a student. Like ever. Lunch was a whole two hours away so he couldn't have been there to take her anywhere. And had she known he was creeping by my office she probably would've thought it was me inviting him. Do you know the lengths he had to go through to come to disturb me in the first place? The building is bursting with students preparing for finals and trying to get whatever extra money they can to carry out the next semester. And here you go with your non-important ass waltzing into a back office to show your face because you think you can get a rise out of me." Finally, she took a breath.

Sinking into the sofa, Nile tried to listen to the details, being cognizant of her emotions. But his own emotions were doing a number on him. "Do you miss him?"

"Oh no! Once I got free, I had time to review all our so-called togetherness and realized I was in a relationship while he was in a situation. That alone shut and longing I had down. And I'm sorry I just went on like a babbling brook about the stupid encounter. You must think I'm a mess."

"I think you're cute. But I need to know where you're at with him so I can strategize on how to take him out of the picture." *I hope she doesn't think I'm going to kill him. But shiidt, if he keep popping up on her at work I might have to.*

She giggled. "For a while I was sad. But not because of wanting him to be back in my life. Just the hurt of someone being so cruel. It's hard to get the image of some other woman getting her guts filled in your own bed with the man you thought to have loved you. Pride had me hiding beneath the covers for months, not wanting to show my face. So, then I became even more pissed that I let him have that kind of impact. If that's too long-winded of an answer, no, I do not miss him. Besides, my sister Camilla, would have him decapitated and then serve his brains as Christmas chitlins if she thought he still had me by the heart."

Her answer was reassuring. Nile chuckled to hide his relief. "Oh yeah? Protective big sis, huh? You got any brothers?" It was also important to get any additional lays of the land.

"Sort of. My sister's husband is the closest thing, but you can't tell him he's not the real deal. Since they met back in High School, he's been family. He is crazy protective, but if he isn't loyal to my sister's happiness, then I don't know what to call him. By extension of his dedication to her, he looks out for me and my Mom, too. His discernment is crazy. He never liked Gordon." Her musings were bashful, innocent.

"Men typically read other men pretty well. It's women that are the mystery. But you, I don't know. You don't strike me as someone who bothers to mask her feelings. I like that. This Gordon character definitely failed."

A sweet laugh shuffled out of her lips, nudging his loins. "It's crazy because he hurt me. I mean it was bad. My soul agonized. The world became blurry. Not even Caprice's violation pained me so much, but his. We had a home together, or so I thought. And now he can't just let me live in peace. It's been a minute since someone has caught my eye." She paused as if to reflect on something she remembered.

"Anyway, they can't have my power and that's probably killing the both of them. That's why I kept my cool. She's dumb and he's a jerk. Match made in heaven, I guess. But now that I've foolishly rambled on about the two of them, if you'd like to run fast and far away, I totally get it."

"Actually, I don't think you do, get it. Your freedom to say whatever you're thinking is refreshing. I'd never have to guess. As a man, that makes my job easy."

Her tone softened. "Oh, I see. What job is that?"

"Whatever you'd hire me for as long as it pleases you." He knew it sounded lame, but it was true.

Man, if she needed me as a friend to listen to her thoughts, I'd donate both of my ears. Although, he hoped for something more hands on. Nile licked his lips. He was beginning to crave her presence. Picturing the way her thighs refused to hide; her boots sliding over those juicy calves; he wanted to let her flow on about her day, while he removed them then proceeded to lay her on the couch and rest her feet across his lap. He'd pull all the tension out of her toes before he'd commence to making them curl. All she had to do was say the word.

"Well, Mr. Ledger." Her tone hinted at sensual curiosity. "All the jobs are quite empty and available right now. So, how about you show me the makings of you? Let me get a good look at your resume and we can take it from there."

"Hmph." Nile thought about his requirement to report back to Anada and the girls the results of their conversation. They had him on the ropes, without a doubt. But he'd be lying if he said he didn't enjoy having a cheering section. *They'd be pretty good wingmen for date night too, I'm sure.* Deciding there wouldn't be a better time, he asked, "Were you planning to go to Friday Night at Sweet Thangs?"

"I wasn't. It kind of seemed like an event you'd attend with a date. As previously mentioned, there's no one on my line."

Maaaan, if she was looking for someone on her line, I'd draw the line, race up and down it, and then erase it just to redraw it so that she would see my hello was the only line she'd ever need. "Would you count me as someone?"

"Should I?"

"You should. But let me make this clear, so there's no second guessing when I pull up on you."

She chuckled. "Oh, you about to pull up. Well, let me get my bumper ready." She was just as corny as he was. As she seemed impressed with her attempt at humor, she was oblivious to the images igniting his urges. Cracking herself up, she snorted and then quieted.

Nile grunted. Mention of her backside caused his little man to jump, yearning for the opportunity to explore her. If only she knew he thought it was admirable how easy it seemed to make her laugh. It was becoming evident to him, any sound she'd let slip from her lips enticed him.

Continuing, Nile laid his groundwork. "I don't like to waste time. Before we go any further, I need to ask if you're seeing someone. I know you gave me your info, and you told me there wasn't anyone on your "line," but I want to make sure there isn't some other guy getting his heart broken by you. My mother always told me to ask it plainly, so there's no room for misinterpretation."

There was silence as if she was contemplating her reply. Another full five seconds and he thought he had lost her. But just as he was getting to call her name, she spoke.

"My heart has been broken, but I've never broken any other to my knowledge. To be honest, I'm probably still a little fragile. My trust in humanity was tarnished with my last relationship. I'm not even sure I know what to do with the likes of someone as bold as you." With the call on speaker, her words filled the room.

"You sound as nerve-wrecked as I am. It's probably a good sign that's what we're doing to each other. There's quite a few things you're doing to me, Miss Joi." Sliding his hand down the front of his sweats, it was now necessary to adjust himself. Somehow the honesty in her spiel had him wanting to take her to unthinkable highs. Intoxicate her to the point where she'd forget all of her lows.

"At the drop of a dime, you're authentic, sincere. Don't doubt yourself when you're with me. So far with all that I've heard, it seems like everything you are is good with me. My faith in humanity has been shaken a time or two, as you can imagine in my line of work. But we won't talk about that tonight. What I will do, is quit being a punk and ask you out already. Joi, would you like to be my date on Friday night?"

Forcing herself to become serious, she replied, "More than anything."

"Great! Because Anada and the little sistahs would kill me if I failed at getting you to go. Those girls been on my ass about you. Like I need someone battery packing me to let me know how remarkable you are."

"Wow! Remarkable? You're about to have me in the mirror doing my dance," she teased.

Another dose of that laugh and he'd for sure be in love.

"I didn't think you were that close to Ms. Anada and her team. You talked to them about me? How do you even know them?"

"Anissa's great-aunt works with me down at the precinct. She's the one who told me about Sweet Thangs' grand opening. I've been frequenting ever since. Thank God too, because it's where I first laid eyes on you."

"So, you believe in God?"

Nile glided over to the kitchen, reached in the refrigerator, and took a water bottle from the twelve pack on the shelf. He took a swig. Glancing at the counter, he pictured her sitting atop, dressed in one of his uniform shirts, asking the most basic of questions. If only she could be there for him to wrap his arms around her waist. He'd answer each with a kiss to her neck until her inhibitions became unguarded. He'd have to wait for such gratification, though. Whatever speed she'd need him to travel, he was committed to go. There was no chance he was going to let this budding togetherness fall from his grip.

"I do believe. My parents also have me believing in speaking desires into existence, fate, and all kind of stuff." He peeked over at the framed picture of his parents beside the television, noting he should probably move it somewhere less pronounced. *Probably not the best example of me being a grown man.*

"Interesting. They've done a great job raising you it appears. My beliefs aren't far off. Sounds like your parents would get along well with my Mom and Uncle."

"Maybe one day they'll have reason to meet. My mother loves cooking and embarrassing me. I think she'd love you too."

"Mr. Ledger, you're pretty presumptuous, but I'll take it. Keep talking all those future plans to me and you may not be able to get rid of me. Are you ready for that?"

Gulping down the remainder of his water bottle, Nile was working to keep his aroused member from jumping through the phone with thoughts of resting its head on her thighs before carving his name on her walls.

"The question is, are you? 'Cause once you let me in, Joi, I ain't leaving until you tell me to."

ROCK candy

At the center of her dressing room, Joi studied herself in the mirror. Even though she stood a good five inches above five feet when she was wearing heels, she felt short and frumpy. Navy-blue jeans hugged her thighs, threatening to reveal the cut of her body shaper. She searched for a poncho that would hide the recent cake bulge of her belly, but to no avail. *And to think, I actually skipped the chocolate this week. Well, not totally.*

Infatuated, she allowed her mind to drift, recounting Nile, his handsomeness, and his demeanor during their initial phone conversation. *One look and he had me hooked. Hearing his deep delivery at night just solidified it. Couldn't tell him though. I mean, I need to leave something up to his imagination. Since Monday, I've spent every night telling him every detail of my life just to keep the bass of his voice as company. I wonder if I have addictive personality?*

"You there? Did you go somewhere to space again?" Camilla blared through the FaceTime speaker. "Homeboy got your mind all twisted. He better be on the up and up. After trolling his social media, he might be alright. He don't spend too much time on there so that's good. Means he has something else to do with his time.

Terrence is looking into his background. Results should be back shortly. I'll text you when they're ready."

Joi huffed as she went through yet another sweater choice that wouldn't fit as she envisioned. The lavender rib used to be her favorite. But since Gordon's departure, it had found its way to up under her bosom, tucking in the creases of her back rolls a little too comfortably.

"Girl, are you still searching for something to wear? The man will be at your door in thirty minutes. Throw on a sweater dress and be done with it. You think he ain't notice whatever extra padding you got going on? He like that cake as much as you do. Owww!" She stuck her tongue out, then wagged it with her arm waving in the air. Poking her booty out, she added a bounce.

"I'd like to think I pack it up pretty efficiently. Besides, he's all buff and what not. Don't guys like that prefer women who keep up an exercise regimen or at least eat clean?" Joi eyed the amber sweater dress she had flung onto the futon.

Every time she had seen Nile, it was in a dress. *He probably thinks I'm some sort of prude that doesn't wear pants. If the rest of my body was as dope as my butt, I'd have less of an issue.* Chin over her shoulder, she studied her bottom through the mirror. After Joi hit thirty, it was the only asset that had remained firm and upright in her opinion. *The gym might not be such a bad idea.*

"There is an audience for every damn body, honey. That man ain't been sitting up on the phone with you every night 'cause he ain't sure. As fine as he is, I'm sure he got every single lady officer at the precinct leaving numbers in his locker. Shoot, I like his vibe and how he on it. Been spitting that old school panty wetter game at you. Let me find out we finally bout to get some new family. Terrence could use a brother. Bruce is probably sick of him by now."

Joi was bubbling over. The excitement for her date had returned. Camilla had a way with words. Often Joi would swear she belonged on a stage as a motivational speaker or on a reality television series. She could incite a riot, or party depending on what came out of her mouth. Either way, she could back it up. *Shame that she hates the shows that would probably make her famous.* She'd always complain that watching people bicker gave her anxiety.

Yanking the sweater dress, Joi pulled it over her head. It fell over her hips and down to her ankles. It hugged the right treasures and made her breasts look like she had enhancements done by a Hollywood doctor with a long list of credentials. Off the shoulder, the dress was perfect for the onyx stoned choker her mother gifted her last Christmas. Once added, she was pleased with how her cocoa butter creamed skin gleamed, as if it demanded touching.

"It would be nice, but I don't want to scare him away by being too thirsty. Whenever I hear his voice I start spilling from my folds." Before Joi could go into further explanation there was a knock at her apartment door.

"Oh, damn. Is that him?"

Camilla sang, "Wow! And he's early. I need to meet this dude."

Joi skipped out of the dressing room, down the hall and through the living room. Pressing her eye over the peephole, she enthusiastically asked who it was. The man standing in her line of vision along with his reply was not what she would've predicted.

"Open up, Joi. It's Gordon, my love."

He was sure of himself. Since she moved out of the apartment they shared, he had never let on that he knew where she lived. Joi contemplated if she should call the police. Afterall, she hadn't given him permission to be at her residence and he did take out a restraining order against her.

"What are you doing here?"

He moved closer to his end of the hole. Eye to eye, he commanded, "Let me in. You know you want to."

"Hold up! Is that who I think it is?" Camilla shouted her disbelief.

Fumbling the phone, Joi didn't know who to respond to first. "Girl, let me call you back."

"Oh, hell to the no you won't. Tell him if he doesn't move from your door, I'm coming to cut his balls off with a chainsaw and if he tries to defend himself, I'll have Terrence put him out of his misery for good."

Gluing her eye back to the opening, Joi voiced her sibling's opinion. "You hear that? Camilla's not playing with you. And for that matter, neither am I. Carry yourself somewhere before there be a real problem here."

He snickered, "Can you honestly say you don't miss me?" What used to be his signature inflection of seduction, corrupted the air. "I know *she* does. Let me come in and wake her up." His grin was less alluring than she remembered.

About-faced, she took a deep breath, hoping he'd take heed to her missing eye. Letting him ruin her rendezvous was not going to happen. Edges needed to be laid, lipstick was waiting to be applied, and her lashes longed for a curl.

Halfway down the hall, Joi tossed her echoing reply behind her. "You are not missed. Now go away." She paused. *Is he leaving?*

To her dismay, he weighted his body against the door. "You don't mean that," he called after her. "I still know how to pick a lock. You used to like that. Could never stay mad at me for too long. You'd lock yourself in the bathroom and before nightfall..."

"Excuse me brother." The thick, thundering, grit of Nile's voice was unmistakable. "Are you handling something, or you mind if I knock?" There was a shuffling of feet as one set gave way to the other.

The bold rapping solidified her suspicion. Nile had indeed arrived. "Oh crap!" A thumping heart and a racing mind made for triggered sweat glands. She fanned herself then glanced at the framed, hanging mirror beside the family photo of her, Mama, Uncle Bruce, Camilla, Terrence, and Kitty. *I can't just leave him out there until I'm ready. And what about Gordon? Is he still out there? Dammit, Gordon. Had me fooling with you at the door all this time and I could've been putting on my makeup.*

Joi's two fishtail braids were gelled neat from when she meticulously twisted them that morning. *But my baby hairs looking like weed lawn. Doggonit! Damn look at these lips. Not even moisturized. I'm so not ready.*

"Would you tell me what the hell is happening, Joi?"

It was then that she was reminded she had left the phone with Camilla listening in, at the foot of the door.

"Do I need to come over there? T is in the driveway as we speak. All it takes is a damn whistle and we'll be there. You already know how he feels about his baby sis."

Darting back over to the front of the apartment, Joi grabbed the phone and whispered into it. "No, I think I might actually be okay. Nile is here. I'll call you back." Catching the tail end of her sister's grunt, Joi found herself pacing.

Nile persisted, knocking again. "Joi? It's me, Officer Ledger. You good?"

Opening up to the smooth mocha officer's towering frame, she melted at the sight of him. He wore a black ski hat that had the right amount of tilt, giving way to one of his soul-searching eyes. With a toothpick lodged in the corner of his mouth, he gritted is pearly white teeth and smirked. Whatever insecurities she had, dissipated with the presence of his approving glare. His jet-black peacoat draped, covering his shoulders yet still exposing his brawn. She found herself wanting to slip her hands into the opening and finding her way deep into his space. Restraint was a task.

"Now that you're here, I am slightly more than good. Would you like to come in a sec?"

Turning to face Gordon's open-mouth, dumbfounded expression, Nile smirked. "Sure. I'd most definitely like to enter."

As Joi shut the door behind them, Nile wasted no time inquiring about the man on the other side of the door. The question hadn't even all the way dived off of the tip of his tongue before she answered. "I told you, won't let me live."

"Hmmm." He scratched his chin. Suddenly snatching Joi by the waist, he held her close to him as he leaned against the wall. "It doesn't sound like he's left." He trailed a single finger along her jawline. Leaning in, he pecked her cheek. Then her collar bone.

By the third kiss, he was nearing her cleavage. Shaking knees advised her if she let him continue, she'd beg him not to stop. "Mr. Ledger," she whispered. "Are you being petty?"

His raspy reply sent a pool to her abdomen. "You want me to quit it?"

Hell nah. I want you to take whatever heaven stick you got that's poking my thigh out and slide that thing so deep in me, I want to think I swallowed it. "Um, no?"

He paused anyway. Staring her in the eyes, he followed with, "After all you've been through, I figured you were owed the right to be petty. But it is my bad. I should've asked for the privilege. You just look so damn good. Please forgive me." Gently he tugged at one of her braids.

Joi stared as she mentally counted down from ten. Contemplating what would be next was bolting electricity through her veins. She pictured them merging their souls in one gut-digging euphoria that would have her singing old spirituals. *We literally have only been talking on the phone for a week. Not even a whole one. And I'm here thinking about letting this man all up in me.* She chewed her inner cheek. *But I'm grown. Who is he going to tell that it would matter to me? I need the dust knocked off of this parched thing anyway. Please Officer, come in and end this drought.*

Stepping to the side, Joi peeked out of the peephole. No Gordon. Whatever was the first thud against the wall she assumed was probably what defeated him. He wouldn't stick around for a real ego bruising. *Not when he could go home to Caprice and hang her from the ceiling with her over-indulging self.* If she knew anything about Mr. Thibodeau, he needed his pride stroked. *His only reason for coming by my home was the same for coming by my office. It had been too long since he'd been able to see the control, he had over me.* She was over him and that he couldn't let sit.

Now by Nile's side, Joi looked over at him with her mind made up. "Make no mistake, I want every inch of you."

He held her hand. "Keep talking."

"However, I don't want all of this because I want to punish him. So, I'm going to finish getting dressed and you're going to take me on this date. Because even if I let you into the depths of my cave, it's not going to be on an empty stomach." She winked.

A smile crept across his lips as he nodded. Reluctantly, Nile unhooked her fingers from his. Walking her way down the hall, Joi was intentional in her sway. She had no idea if she would be able to take ownership of his heart, but the way his kisses were etching themselves into her memory, she was going to take her nature and wrap it around his mind if for nothing else, for the rest of the night.

MOON *pie*

As Nile's vehicle approached the parking lot, he was excited for Anissa and Vashti. Instantaneously, the success of their "Friday Night at Sweet Thangs," could be determined. Patrons were lined outside of the door, awaiting their chance to be seated. Loudspeakers boasted the jazzy tunes crooning from the inside. Everyone appeared jovial.

Joi's eyes danced with appreciation as well. It had been a while since she enjoyed such a festive scene. The white Christmas lights draped over the windows and the couples with genuine laughter ringing through the air was enjoyable to look at, better yet to be a part of. And if that weren't enough, she was there with a man who sent tremors to her core simply by saying her name.

Wondering how the young women had transformed the space to accommodate such a crowd, Nile snatched his chained badge from the cupholder and placed it around his neck. Roaming his eyes over his ravishing date, he asked, "You ready?" Her subtle nod had him biting down on his lips, doing his best to tame the fireworks in his veins.

Hand in hand, he and Joi made their way to the front. Nile didn't know what to expect when he pulled up to Joi's apartment complex earlier. It was a given she'd look good enough to abandon all plans and lay her where she stood. Whenever he was able to catch a glimpse of her, his groin became heavy. What he didn't think was that he would not only come face to face with her ex-boyfriend but feel compelled to show him how much of a non-factor he was about to become. Once his lips felt the tenderness of her skin, if she would've let him, he would have hoisted her up on that wall and plowed his future away inside of her. Her scent was like a ripe fruit basket, ready for eating. Yet, he wanted her even more when she insisted that they continue with the agenda and head out to Sweet Thangs. A woman who had requirements was one that excited him and got his imagination active with making plans for the future.

"Nile, you made it," Sheryl enthusiastically greeted.

She kissed his cheek. Then flashing a rejoiceful smile, and swiveling over to Joi, she noted, "And you must be the hot date I've heard so much about. My girl, Anissa is very much enamored with this thing between the two of you blossoming."

Joi was radiant. Her cheeks blushed and eyes squinted. "You're very sweet, thank you. Anissa is definitely a fave."

"It's such a great turnout. The tent seating out back with the poetry paintings are already filling up." Patting the backside of her blonde wig, Sheryl continued to marshal the couple in.

Melodies accompanied by light and gleeful murmuring serenaded their entrance. Confection aromas begged for them to come in further. Pridefully, Nile took in the ambience. The team had managed to clear the floor, creating a circle of seating. And then they created a makeshift stage in the middle. Each table was one made for two. Glassed votive candles adorned each setting, coupled with a single flower whose color differed from the next. A perfect contrast to the chocolate colored tablecloths.

Joi peered up at Nile. She tightened her grip around his fingers. The twinkle in her eye signaling, whatever path he was on with her, was the right one. Receiving his smirk, let her know he hadn't truly taken her down the road just yet, but once he did, she'd be clear about the arrival.

Seeing as though the vibe was non-combative, Nile removed his badge. There was no need to have anyone under pressure. Everyone in attendance was there to have a good time and there probably wasn't one person in the city who would disrespect Anada Moore's shop. Her name rang bells in the toughest of circles as well as the most elite. Sweet Thangs possessed the magic of being neutral ground.

Anada and her husband were seated at a table near the back. As she gazed into his eyes, he fed her chocolate dipped pineapples, licking his lips while watching each bite she took. It was either going to be a short night or a long night for the two of them, depending on who was assessing it. They were completely oblivious to the younger couple's entrance and Nile was filled with longing for a similar situation. However, with Joi by his side he concluded that it was only a short time away.

Nile kept his voluptuous date near as they glided to an open table at the tip of the circle. Once he helped her remove her mustard colored, floor-length, waterfall overcoat, it was hard not to notice heads turn her way. The way her hips rounded; you'd have to be blind not to watch her movements without foaming at the mouth.

"Damn, these lights got you glowing. I don't know how long we can stay because behaving is going to be one hell of a job for me," Nile confessed.

Gulping, Joi thanked Vashti for bringing out the menus and glasses of water. Once they were rid of the company, Joi found her retort. "If I'm being transparent, I was thinking the same. But we both know how much I love chocolate cake." She giggled.

Watching her face sparkle as she browsed the menu options, Nile was motivated to get her burgundy lipstick to caress each of his tattoos. *Now I totally understand why dudes be out here getting their girl's lips branded on their body. But dammit, her face without makeup, when I arrived at her place, was just as provocative.* He shifted his weight, whispering to his pipe to remain at ease. Detecting his leer, she trapped her tongue between her teeth, then looked up and winked. *Okay, keeping my hands off of her is going to damn near kill me. I can't even look away from her for too long. She's probably going to be my wife.*

Perusing the list of drinks paired with desserts, Nile was impressed. Looking over items that demanded to be tasted by the mind before the tongue, he couldn't decide if he'd order the Rum and Done Chocolate Punch with the German Sugar Squares or the Tiny Tequila with the Lemon Brownie Corners. In the background, the MC was introducing the poet, Jess Words.

Joi had placed her menu on the table. Looking around, she too was taken aback by the shop's transformation. They had closed the doors, announcing they would be admitting more after ten. "Damn, they got enough business to take customers in waves. That's so crazy. They're going to be at it all night." Recognizing the ease in which her words could be misconstrued she paused, widening her eyes and tucking in her bottom lip. "Okay, so I think I will order the Orange Vodka with of course a slice of Dark Bark Chocolate Cake," she concluded, switching the subject.

Nile nodded then searched for Vashti. Catching sight of Anissa, he grinned at her excited dash over. *This ought to be interesting.*

"O-M-G! You guys look so good together. Joi, I ain't ever seen your hair in braids, but you are rocking them joints, boo. Oh wait, they're fishtails. Yes, honey. And Nile, you already know, with your big ole Hershey ass," she joked.

Giving Anissa their orders, Joi peered at the handsome specimen sitting across from her. The poet's words in the background, it was as though they had their own narration.

"Don't fight it;
slip deeper into your addiction.
For chocolate lovers are different.
Sticking and melting;

calling for caution
to be thrown to the wind..."

Breaking the heating tension, Joi prodded, "So, Nile, tell me about your experience in this community. I know you were transferred here on purpose. Is it what you hoped it would be, or do you feel like you've increased your chances of danger?"

Nile took a second to ponder his response. The last time he had a conversation about his intent, it veered so far to the left that he decided to end its course. He could only hope this one would not suffer the same demise.

"Actually, it's moving in the right direction for me, most of the time. When I'm doing my real job, the kids feel safe. I get the elders to smile. Some of the dudes out on the corner welcome me to chat it up with them for a few. Probably because most of the time I was without a partner. They're less intimidated. I would like to think I've gotten them to think twice about whatever trouble they'd consider getting themselves into. Is there crime, yes, but I don't want you to have your glasses colored by what the news or stereotypes provide." He awaited her take on his point of view. His heart running a marathon, he hoped her own views wouldn't be far off at the opposite end of the spectrum.

"Wow! Your outlook is pretty impressive. I feel like your goals are admirable and not much different from mine. It's why I've been working so long at the college. My way of contributing to our neighborhood is helping those who think they can't afford a higher education. I've been considering my own enterprise recently. Something small but impactful, you know? Counsel folks who won't even step foot in a school because they don't believe. Help them see their possibilities."

She met his smile with a subtle gaze. As much as he was thanking his lucky stars to have finally found someone to confide his inner passions in, so was she. Two fanciful idealists daring to step foot in one another's dreams.

Taking her time to find the words to break her concentration away from his full-sized lips, she twiddled with her fingers. "I for one think ideals are what we should strive for. Your attempt to be part of the healing for our people gives you a special layer. Honestly, it's a blessing you'd even share that with me. 'To truly change how the police see us, we must become the us, of the police.' That's what Uncle Bruce always says. He's retired now but he's a big advocate of black and brown police officers. Hell, he'd probably dub you son-in-law once I tell him you're a design from the same cloth."

Playing coy, Nile replied, "Yeah? And what would you dub me as?"

Her temperature rising, Joi paused. The glow of his rich skin and the intensity in which he dove headfirst into tackling her thoughts, set fire to her thighs. Swiping her tongue across her lips she responded, "Anything you're trying to be. But please don't keep coming for me like this if you're not willing to go some rounds. I can dig tonight and I'm down to have a fabulous time with you, all night. However, getting me to open up to possibilities of long term when that's not what you're looking for, is unfair and immature."

Whatever bum-ass dude she had before got her all twisted up in the mind. She's crazy if she thinks I'm afraid of her. Nile leaned in. "Believe me when I say, if nothing else, I'm intentional. When I ask you to open up, it's because I want in." He sat back, letting his words find their way into her system.

Clearing her throat, Joi nodded. Flushed, she used her hand to fan herself. The only word she could muster was, "Whew!"

Dessert was served by Anissa. This time she hadn't the time to go off on a tangent as there were multiple orders waiting to be basked in. Appreciating the supply of delights that was set before them, Nile was now certain he was sharing this moment with his forever.

Eager to continue their conversation, Nile offered, "My father always said life has to have a purpose. And if that purpose isn't to better more than just yourself, then you've found the wrong one. Pick again."

He savored the taste of the rum. The kick was enough to get him feeling nice after one glass, but the sweetness that infiltrated his taste buds had him considering a second. He took another sip as he considered his plight. *She has no idea how serious about her I really am. But that's cool. I'm more of the show type anyway.*

She handed him his napkin then spread hers across her lap. "Is that what your father says? It sounds like you come from an amazing foundation. You've certainly captivated me. When I first laid eyes on your beautiful face, I hadn't fathomed you'd have so much depth. Tell me more, Mr. Ledger." Indulging in her first bite of the decadent cake, she closed her eyes as though she was on her first journey to bliss.

His heart paused. *Well that's a first. She thinks I'm beautiful. Got me all the way in my feelings like I'm some chick being hit on.* It began to beat again when he peeped her hold onto her cinnamon straw between two fingers and take a long sip of her tonic. Meanwhile, he was envisioning her sampling his manhood the same. With her eyes big and bright, he recalled her request for more.

"What can I tell you that I haven't all week? You've gotten more out of me than those trauma therapists the department makes us see."

She tilted her head, considering the truth of his remark. "Touché. And same. I swear I've spilled every bean I've got." Landing another morsel of cake onto her tongue, she seemed to be transporting into another galaxy.

"Baby, this thing is so rich," she cooed. "It is amazing. Would you like some?" She took a bigger swig, washing down the delicacy.

"You sure? I mean, I don't know if it's okay to deprive you of any of that happiness you've got going on over there." He looked on as she furrowed her brow and coated her throat with what was left in her glass.

Apparently, she's a lightweight. Nile observed Joi's cheeks coloring as if there was a heated oven beneath them. He took another gulp of his rum. *I'm glad she's having fun though.*

Seductively, she squinted and rested her elbows on the table. "Do you mind if I feed you some of my happiness?" Lifting her fork, she guided it to his lips.

Opening up, he allowed her to supply him with a taste. He kept watch of her fierce focus as he chewed. She used her thumb to gingerly finger away a bit of fudge icing from his lips. When she licked said cream from her digit, all his patience had expired. In spite of the cake being every bit as good as she promised, this set-up was no longer going to work for Nile.

As Joi was reaching over the table into his plate to try Nile's untouched chocolate, her plump rear rising off her chair, body looking like it was about to arch, he grabbed her wrist. Her heated glare as intense as his, she waited for him to take the lead.

Still with her wrist in his grasp, Nile dug into his pocket and tossed a few twenties on the table, shoved a brownie bite into Joi's mouth, and commanded, "Let's go." Without a second blink she grabbed her coat and obliged.

DIPPED CHOCLOATE
fondue

"Yours," Joi exclaimed while allowing herself to me led by the hand, out of the venue. Relishing in Nile's unyielding clutch of her fingers, her insides were sweltering.

Nile's uncanny ability to understand the one-word demand was indeed a direction, and for him to head straight to his abode was an added match to her fire. It also secured her. Letting her know he most likely wasn't hiding a family or a crazy live-in girlfriend. His only response was the clenching of his jaw and the replacement of his toothpick.

After helping Joi into the passenger seat, Nile jogged around to his side. He hopped in behind the wheel without a word. The mood setting playlist still singing through the car speakers tempted their caged desires. He kept his eyes on the road for the six blocks they travelled before pulling into his section of renovated townhomes.

Silencing the engine, Nile remained diligent. He missioned on out of the car, sprung to his front door, unlocked it, and then came back to let Joi out. Opening the car door, he held his hand out for her to take.

Did he just unlock the door so that I wouldn't stand in the cold?

Where did this man come from? Honey, I don't know but he's certainly going to cum from me tonight.

The minute the pair were on the other side of the door, he pinned her arms against the wall. Keeping himself at arms distance, his expression was piercing, yet sincere. Wasting no time, he got to his point. "I'm not about to play with you. All I need is a yes. I want to eat you, touch you, fill you, unravel you, and lift you all over again. Whoever said you wasn't a mother-fucking problem, lied to you. If I have to write the word, beautiful all over your womb for the rest of the night, I will, if that's what it would take to convince you. But I ain't going nowhere you're unsure about going."

I think I just came. Catching her bottom lip beneath her teeth, she nodded.

He eased his force and brought his body in close. Kissing her nose and then her cheek, he asked, "Is that a yes?" A kiss to her other cheek came with the warmth of sweet rum on his breath.

One new whiff of his woodsy balm and her feminine leak would soon leave her dehydrated. She pressed her lips against his. Tasting the remnants of fudge icing on his tongue, she cupped his face, sucking him in. His lips surrounding hers, the anticipation of his lower bulge seeking comfort inside of her, forged the temptation to drop to her knees.

Nile's hands gripped her hips like he had taken possession of them once before. Pulling his mouth from hers he affirmed, "I have to hear you say it. Tell me yes and I will consume you." He tapped his fingers against her backside.

She managed to get ahold of enough of her senses to provide a whispery, "Yes." Finding that she was levitating due to his strength, she included, "And stay as long as you like."

With a grunt, he pulled her dress up over her thighs while pressing himself against.... "What's this?" He felt around.

Joi gulped. She coughed her throat clear. "Umm, a body shaper."

"Man, take this shit off." He lowered her legs. After unzipping each of her boots and removing them from her feet, he peeled the garment down to her ankles.

As she stepped out of the puddled fabric, her palms began sweating. Her excitement was dissolving. She took a deep breath. Recalling Gordon's supposed pet name of her fupa, she thought, *Here comes, "Fat Belly."* Her panties were coming off, but as bad as she wanted him, she found herself cowering.

"Relax. I can feel the tension in your limbs." He glided his index between her folds then tasted his finger. "I want to show you something."

Nile lifted her amber covering over her head then unlatched her lacey brassiere. Intertwining his fingers with hers, he took the lead into his living room where there was a full-length mirror leaned against the far corner. He stood her before it. Still fully dressed, he stepped behind Joi, his hands roaming her skin until they found their way to her midsection. He took hold of the flap of a stomach pouch while setting his eyes to look through the mirror, into hers, locking into her soul.

"Listen to me," he said while nibbling at her earlobe. "You could lose this, keep this, grow this, whatever. I'm still going to rub it, kiss it, and suck on it. One day, if you'd have me, I'd put my seeds in it. And after that sample of juice I just had, I'd do it every night if you let me. You got me?"

Matching his glare, the esteem conjuring inside her was overwhelming. *Girl, you better not shed a damn tear.* All of the floods were welling. She did the only thing she seemed to be able to do since she walked through the door, nod. Biting down on his lip, he spun her around. As she faced him, he snatched his ski-hat off and tossed it. Removing his coat, he did the same with it. Slowly, he unbuttoned his fuchsia plaid button down, exposing the most mesmerizing, dark chisel she had ever been exposed to. Once his shirt was removed, he unbuckled his belt.

Overcome with heat, Joi ventured forward and unzipped his

jeans. With the best of intentions, she steered them down to his feet, her stature lowering along with them. Helping him out of the denim and then his boxers, Joi remained on her knees. Beholding his swollen member as it teetered, she inspected its generous length. Licking her lips, she was compelled to take a second to admire the beauty in its big-headed curve.

However, Nile had his own agenda. Before she could open her mouth to bless him with her appreciation, he had knelt to meet her, then lowered his head to her neck. He tipped her chin back as he commenced to planting kisses. Massaging her breasts with his large hands, he laid her down. "Me, first," he rumbled.

Sliding down to her oyster, he made no detour getting to her pearl. He breathed her skin in, getting to her core, as he sucked with precise pressure. With one hand he held her at her base, pulling her nearer when she was inclined to pull away. Mindful of the moisture her lips generated, he took pause to slurp them temporarily dry but then return to the tip of her peak.

Sensations firing through her being, she flexed her fingers. Massaging her own breasts, Joi's sensuality was coming alive. No longer able to withstand the pleasure of his devouring and fiddling with her nipples, she gripped his shoulders. *What kind of... Oh my goodness...* Her breaths became staggered as she arched her back. An explosion mounting inside of her, she whimpered.

His soul milking suction tapering off into deep, wet, passionate kisses, he confidently warned, "You're going to cum. It's going to be hard, but I want all of it. Everything you feel, let me have."

There was no bigger truth that what he gave as prophecy. Joi's rain was an uncontrollable storm. He lapped, massaged, then slipped a finger between her bottom cheeks and entered where she had never let anyone. Tenderly, he twisted his finger in her backdoor while her front was rebuilding for another squall. The euphoria escalated with his encouragement.

"Don't hold it. But tell me if you want me to stop."

"Never stop." She wound her hips in rhythm with his pleasuring. "You can have all of me," she purred. And then without control over the words pouring from her lips, she begged, "Take it. Oh my... I ain't' ever felt..." The second bomb was ticking away.

"Hmmm," he hummed. "You taste better than anything on that menu. Give me that shit."

Her body was compelled to obey. The second detonation was accompanied by her knees quaking and toes contorting. Sill with his finger coaxing the aftershock into a drizzle, he stared at her.

"You're even more beautiful when you're in the throes of a nut. I'm going to free my hand, slowly. Let me know if anything hurts."

In one swoop he had freed his finger and lifted her into his arms. As if she were his bride or an incapacitated loved one, he carried her naked body up the carpeted stairs for the sole purpose of taking what they started to the next level in his bedroom. He wanted to etch the sensation of ecstasy into her body. Make her believe his bed and the bliss tingling through her organs were joined at the hip. When she entered her won room, she'd recall his and decide to rush back. Once he placed her at the center of his king-sized bed, he disappeared into the private bath.

Joi listened as she could hear the water running. Remaining quiet, her thoughts wondered. *That's not the shower.* Listening closely, she determined it was the sink and made the assumption he was washing his hands. *If I could, I would get up and clean too, but honestly, I'm still trembling.*

Emerging from the restroom with a washcloth, Nile accompanied his conquest. As if she were bedridden and he was her nurse, he used the warm washcloth to freshen her center. Simultaneously, he kissed her belly button.

All his care had her wanting, needing to please him. Watering her mouth was the sight of his third leg keeping at attention. Finally regaining her strength, she sat up. "Now let me."

There was no time for his response. His rod had become her

vehicle of performance and she wouldn't stop until she had put on a full show. His grunts and growls motivated her bob. Tonguing down his stretch, she maintained her hold of him. If she could bring him a fraction of the satisfaction he had given to her, she'd take it as a win.

But no. He wouldn't allow his cream to come down. Instead, he reached into the top drawer of his nightstand. Producing a condom, he used his teeth to tear it open. Gently he nudged her head away, strapped up, and set the rule, "Tap when it becomes too much."

He then gripped her jaw and shoved his tongue into her mouth. Their desires colliding, he flipped her onto her back and lowered himself atop. When he entered the much-desired clutch, Joi couldn't stop herself from stammering his name. With tenacity, he worked his deliberate grind into her spirit. His hands crowned around her face; he mastered her rhythm, staring into her eyes.

"Give me kiss."

She granted him her lips. He inhaled them. Lifting one leg around his waist she permitted him additional access. He thanked her with deeper strokes. Taking his tongue from hers, he buried his head into her skin. His teeth grazed her shoulders. His breaths were like the relief of ocean winds against her ears.

He needed to get another look at her. Pausing for a beat, while continuing to fill her with the force of his branch, he declared, "Joi Briar, I'm going to let you know what love feels like. Open up to me and I promise you, I'm going all the way in. I'll go as deep as you're willing to go, and I won't ever turn away unless you make me."

Hissing her satisfaction, once again she was fighting her tears. She contemplated how he felt so at home. With merely his presence she was full; and then he had an aura that made her feel safe. The fact that he held the skill to send currents through her spine and manipulate them to travel to whichever part of her body he determined, was dozens of cherries on top.

His thrusts commanded her attention as he purposefully gave her his. If everything he said was true, she'd pack her heart up and put it away in his pocket. He could have it.

As her thighs parted the way to more of his girth, she clenched the skin of his neck between her teeth. Then she whispered, "Take everything you're coming for."

JELL-O shots

Joi's essence was engraved into Nile's veins. From the moment he first tasted her lips, she had penetrated his exterior and made herself a home in his bloodstream. After their initial meld, the entire weekend he pleasured in learning how she moved, her desires, her subtleties. Now it was six weeks later, and he was still relishing in the study of her language and all its translations.

Effortlessly, they had become stuck on one another, requiring the designation of all available free time, ensuring there'd be no space unfulfilled. Nights were energetically laced with their laughter, confessions, and sweetheart touches. Mornings began with proactive stress relieving moans as Nile aimed to see her strut through her day, knowing she was cared for. Still unable to get enough of her voice, he called her line every afternoon during his course through the neighborhood. Even video phoning when he'd get the opportunity to break from his partner and stop in to see Anada and the girls. Because after all, they too wanted to invest in her brightness. When she was happy, she was light.

With her head against his chest, Nile peeked at the clock. Despite it being his day off, his organs would awake at five in the morning, before the sun showed its face. The early rising was welcomed. It gave him a chance to view Joi in her slumber. Her zebra print silk bonnet would rarely keep place over her head full of twists. If it weren't for his sunrise surveillance, she'd never know where to find her covering when she'd awake.

"Hmmm," she stirred. "Something feels different this morning. Everything alright?" Feeling for his skin, she wormed her arm across his thigh. "Tell me what's on your mind, Mr. Ledger." Even with her eyes closed she perceived him.

"I was talking to my mother yesterday." He paused, contemplating how much he would share with her.

Disclosing the parts of his intimate life with his parents came on the heels of a slight confrontation with his partner. Officer Gregory would be tricky. She'd be overly concerned with the interaction, which wasn't the true reason he had been quietly thinking.

Despite being only newly assigned, Daniel Gregory, the nuisance of a man, gave himself the go ahead to intrude on what his designated partner took personal, Joi. He talked as if he knew her. It was a move Nile would never embrace and now, he knew it too.

Routinely pulling his cruiser into the parking lot of Sweet Thangs, Nile took notice of its light crowd. Gone were the days where he could pop his head into an empty shop at two in the afternoon. The success of the inaugural "Friday Night" event got the ball rolling on the immeasurable increase. Being the week of Christmas, there were more newcomers looking to take a break from their diets and get hold of a piece of the baked jubilation that was quickly becoming a household name.

"Officer Ledger, nice to see you!" As Anada steamed milk, she snuck in a grin. "Will you get your regular brownie? We do have a special edition chocolate cake this week. Perhaps you can take it to your love. You know since we'll be closed on the holiday." She grinned.

"Speaking of which," Anissa butted in before he could formulate his response. Glancing over at Vashti who was already packaging a slice of the aforementioned cake, they shared a giggle.

"Man, we want to know if you're spending the holiday with your

new, Joi." Leave it to Vashti to boldly step to the plate. It wasn't a day she was alive where she'd have bite marks on her tongue.

Disturbing their playful poking, Officer Gregory sauntered through the door. Along with him, an air of loath and displacement. "Whole department knew I'd be able to find you here. Rumor is this place has got the best sweets this side of town. Must be something to it." Licking his lips, he watched as Anada served her unique brand of cranberry tarts. His joker-like grin soared his level of creep. He joined Nile at the corner of the display casing.

Judging by the hand on Anada's hip in association with Anissa and Vashti's scowls, their brother officer figured he'd say something before Gregory was told where to go and how to get there. Customers were equally discomforted, minimizing small talk and seemingly adding pace to their exits.

"No urgencies came over the radio." Nile gripped the on-the-house, Caramel Prep Anissa placed in his hand.

"Oh, don't look so concerned. We're partners now. You're allowed a little break here and there. Besides, my absence this morning probably had you believing you were riding solo for the day. My fault on that. Had some business to attend to, if you know what I'm saying." He gripped the buckle of his slacks.

Nile eyed the dispersing of the disgusted women. They busied themselves with anything that would carry them away from him. Anada wiped down the counter while Vashti manned the register. Anissa found a calling behind the kitchen door.

"Anyway, I figured shooting over here would give me a good chance to talk to you on your turf, so to speak. There's something personal I'd like to discuss with you, and it really isn't appropriate to do it back at the precinct." As if they were true comrades, Daniel sought understanding in Nile's face. He was under the impression that he would be able to confide, and Nile would be receptive.

With one eyebrow raised, Nile nodded. Distrust plucked at the hairs on his chin. It became imperative to step away. Officer Gregory was the type to be grossly inappropriate, then cop out by labeling whatever dick-wad comments he made, a joke. Nile had already peeped his slithery regard of Anada. If Dylan rolled in there while she was still wearing the look of revolt across her face, the situation could have become complicated.

Leading his new partner out into the parking lot, Nile sighed. "Alright, we're out of earshot of anyone who might care what we're talking about. Or do you prefer to sit in the squad car?"

Daniel Gregory placed his hand on Nile's shoulder. "No, I think we're good here, player." He was proud of his use of the outdated terminology. Once he realized Nile hadn't joined in on the comedy hour, he settled himself. "Seriously. I saw you hanging out with that young woman the other night. The real pretty one with the big hair."

The mention of Joi pounded away at the lover's heart. "What the hell is he worried about Joi for," Nile grumbled. It was unnerving to have this man pick her up on his radar. Although, it would be hard for anyone to ignore how stunning she was. But to have his fellow officer, who still hadn't mastered the fellowship that is supposed to be the force, made his brain rummage through scenarios in which she would need to be kept safe. Immediately. Nile thought to ask her if she had ever shot a pistol before.

"What about Joi?"

"Yes, Joi. That was her name. Oddly ironic, though."

Through gritted teeth, Nile probed. "Daniel, are you getting at something? 'Cause if you are, get to it."

"Right. Listen, we all like our fun. I maybe more than the next guy. But that one. Hmmm. Watch yourself around that little lady. She's one of them barefoot in the streets kind of gals. I don't doubt she's two handfuls." He held his arms out as if he were carrying bags of groceries. "But one of them hands might regret it. She's a little off the rocking horse. Crazy in love turn raging lunatic, you know what I mean," he scoffed.

Nile was aware that if he wasn't careful, his animalistic breathing would give his anger away. Although, what the man was insinuating was enough to redden his tiger eye and have him draw his gun. "No. I don't know what you mean. Why don't you explain." His blood cells were bouncing off of each other.

Containing the kettle of emotions that were near whistling was proving to be impossible. Squaring the Officer in the eyes, Nile replied, "Dude, get this here, you don't know the first thing about Joi. Dropping hints about a damn incident I'm not only aware of, but am in full support of her actions, will do nothing for this so-called partnership of ours." Firmly gripping his collarbone, Nile continued, "If you ever feel the need to mention Joi again, do us both a favor and don't."

Grasping the magnitude of Nile's disdain, Daniel nodded. If it hadn't been for his cell phone vibrating, Nile would've probably dislocated half of Gregory's being, but for now it would have to wait. The one man who could talk him down from the ledge was on his line and the timing couldn't have been more perfect for everyone involved.

"Hey Pops. What's up?"

Jerking Nile from his thoughts was Joi snapping her fingers. "Where'd you go? You're all in your head. It's getting cold out in these sheets."

"My Mom wants to invite you over for our traditional Christmas breakfast." He decided to skip over the venting to his father which led to the invitation from his mother. "Grady, if he's this worked up over the honor of this young woman, she's got to be as special as they come. I know Thanksgiving was too early, but can't we meet her by now? Have her come for breakfast. Or if she isn't an early riser, we can make it a brunch. I need to meet the woman who has my son ready to shoot the moon over her."

"So, is this invitation a good thing?" Joi traveled her fingers down the center of his chest. "Or are you afraid that it may be too soon? The way you're laying here, staring up at the ceiling, I can't tell if this is something you want."

Nile looked down at her half-opened eyes. She was holding her breath for his response. Little did she know, he was the one who tossed all night with swirls of possibilities, preparing for her to back him up, plead for more time, and ultimately turn him down. They had been inseparable from their first night together. Leaving her in the mornings was dreadful for him. His evenings at the gym would be cut short due to his anxiousness to show up at her door and lead her into a world of their making. Never had he been so smitten over a woman. There were possible over the years but none he wanted to take as his wife as assuredly he wanted to take her. If he could've introduced her to his parents and had a ceremony three weeks ago, he would have considered it. So, no, for him it wasn't a moment too soon. But it was her time that mattered him most.

"To be candid, you can meet her right now. She'd dote on you and be in awe of how smart you are. My Pops would be tickled at how adorable your smile is and give me props for finding someone who would let me watch the game without rolling her eyes. I'd be proud to have you sit at the table beside me." He reset her slipping bonnet.

With more zest than Nile could expect from her at such an early hour in the day, she shot up. Her grin was wide as she straddled his lap. "Mr. Ledger, do you know your fearlessness when it comes to us is intoxicating?" She leaned forward. Kisses to his bare chest turned to her reaching for the final condom on the nightstand.

While using her teeth to free the rubber from its wrapping, she added, "My mother and sister have been on me about having you come over on Christmas evening. I told them you'd have your own family traditions. But now look at you, wanting me to take part in them."

Sheathing his shaft, she was taking her time. His pole jumping at the occasion, he watched her steady it with her rouge manicure. Her precision was a seduction all on its own.

He held her hips and adjusted his beneath. "I ain't scared of Joi." His member was fully erected and rapping for an opening. "Don't you be afraid of me. The only way I'm trying to hurt you is by stretching you to take more of my love." His mighty man found his way into the warmth that was the woman he had become addicted to.

Throwing her head back, Joi swirled her bottom, getting herself reacquainted with the mass of his curve. Once she gathered the air in her lungs, she replied, "Now don't you go using words like love. I'm sensitive and liable to take it the wrong way."

Nile palmed her derriere. Separating the halves like ripe papaya, he held them in place. "Take it how you want, but I'm going to tell you how I'm giving it." He rose to meet her gaze. Grabbing her wrists, he was adamant about her needing to know he would not be toying with her. "Joi Anita Briar, I am all the way in love with you."

Feeling her slow rise up, he pulled her back down. Watching her breath hitch, grew him another inch. Slowly, he stirred in her pot while silence mounted between them. He loosened his grip and allowed the carousel that was them to make its music.

Gripping his shoulders, Joi was regaining her control. Her cadence mirrored his. She dared not look away. "You are the most incredible man I have ever met. What I've been feeling for you..." She paused to moan. "I knew it to be love after our first conversation. But I have been trying to convince myself it was impossible." Her teeth sunk into her bottom lip. "Already, I don't want to live without you."

Her confession was like lightening to his spear. One hand around her meaty breast, he sucked and slurped her areola, while the depths he was trying to reach would have him dip into the tip of her heart. She whimpered and he firmed.

"So, you love me?" Full of rasp and hunger, his question was prying her drip.

Sucking in her cheeks, she shuddered. Watchful of all that was behind his windowed soul, she replied, "Yes. I love you, Nile."

All at once, he lifted her by the bottom and threw her down on her back, never exiting her pond. Her wetness poured then squeaked like it was hurting yet begging to be soothed, concurrently. Passion surged through his thighs, elevating his sac. He would earn all of her love over and over again. She would call no other name but his for eternity.

With his thrusts more powerful, her inaudible oohs became solidified squeals. Her bonnet had let go. Twists falling to her face, they became untangled. He guided the hair away from shielding her eyes. No one walking the earth could craft her kind of beauty in his mind. *Only the divine designer could conjure her.* Slowing his pace, he stuck his tongue out. Wrapping hers around his, together they savored their devotion.

Waterfalls drenching the sheets, she clenched her muscles. He was calculated with how he flickered inside of her. "You're mine, Joi. I ain't ever giving you up." Drowning in her rippling sea, he stroked their way home.

Lemon drops

DAYLIGHT HAD MADE ITS RETURN. THE NIGHT BEFORE, WITH all of its holiday frenzy, the city settled about the nine o'clock hour. The energized rush of last-minute shopping and Yuletide caroling subsided into indoor preps and hushing young children off to sleep. Reluctantly, Joi had torn herself away from Nile's rapture. Although he would be working the overnight shift, he had made it plain she was welcome to stay. But her nerves were jumpy. To calm them, it was vital for her to have solitude. *"Everything I need to wrap gifts is at my place. Besides, I still pay rent there."* However, what she truly needed was the time and space to process the slated meeting of his parents.

Now here she was, wide awake, laying with her face to the ceiling. For two and a half hours she had been stuck in the same position with the same ruminations. Sunrays barged through the blinds of her bedroom, reminding her the agreed upon hour was near. *What if his Mom thinks we're moving too fast? Women are the first to judge timing. But can I say I'd be any different? He is her only child. Goodness, that curve of his lips and the silkiness of his skin, heck if he were my son, I'd swear every woman out there was trying to use him for breeding. Really, I'd like to thank her. Nile is one hell of a human.*

Almost too good to exist. But Camilla says she felt this way about falling for Terrence. And was a damn gangster. Although he had his shit with him, it was never a lack of loyalty, love and respect for my sister. And Mama says from day one she was smitten with Uncle Bruce. I wonder who he favors most when we're close up? In their family photo it seems like his Pops. But his spirit, gentleness, and thoughtfulness, now that has to be his Mama's doing. Like she knew she was sending him out into the world to make some woman fall into his abyss. This is all probably some elaborate dream I made up and I'm still in the bed waiting to wake on a lousy Thursday morning. Either way, I haven't been pinched free yet, so I might as well get up and get on with whatever's coming.

With the decision to rise, she dragged through her shower and the brushing of her teeth. But once she made it out of the bathroom, the draft that hit, added a sense of urgency to her movements. Although temperatures outside were in the high thirties, it felt unusually warm for Christmas. Nile would be on his way within the hour. And per usual, she was still undecided on what she would wear.

Taking in the sight of her congested closet, Joi searched for an outfit he had yet to see her in. Thinking back to her latest visit to the church, where she felt as if she was out of uniform, she cringed then blew out a deep breath. *Okay Joi, relax. As long as you don't show up looking like the harlot he prefers at night, we should be fine. Lord, I sound like Camilla.*

Preferring the security of her own vehicle, she volunteered to meet him at his childhood home. At the time, she imagined the possibility of his matriarch being a practicing witch who'd brew a spell to keep her away from her cherished son. *Maybe it's these same thoughts that made Gordon refuse to take me to see his Godmother. After raising him for most of his life, you'd think she'd be dying to meet the woman he was laying up with for the past few years. But given his track record, who's to say she hadn't?*

However, Nile insisted if there was ever a moment when she was compelled to make a run for it; he'd oblige without pushback. Giving in, she was now pressed for time, still prancing around in her unmentionables.

Her first thought was to wear a fall inspired jumper skirt with leggings underneath. Determined not to appear as though she was trying too hard, she then opted out of the leather ball-skirt and boots. She peered at herself in the mirror, deliberating what she wanted Mrs. Ledger's opinion of her to be. Until it dawned on her, "These are the things I cannot control."

So, she went with a garnet cowl neck, waist length sweater over black trousers. Pulling her curls into a low bun, she let a few ringlets drop, accenting the peacock centered hoop earrings Camilla gifted her when she returned from her baecation to St. Croix. After staring at her shoe rack for what was bordering on eternity, she chose a pair of black and white tuxedo pumps. "A good shoe is always the silver lining."

By the time Nile was texting his arrival, she had only her lipstick left to apply. As much as she loved the way her lips perked when adorned with red, she was hesitant. Until, he was at her door knocking and hollering, "Don't second guess yourself. You're always perfect. Now please tell me that you're ready."

Opening the door to her apartment, Joi came face to face with her awaiting beau. "So, what, you're psychic now?" She pretended to be offended.

Designing an escort herself, wouldn't bring her a more handsome vision than the freshly tapered man towering over and reaching for her hand. His biscuit colored fisherman's coat striped with black and maroon along the edges, and matching ski hat contrasted perfectly against his rich skin.

He grabbed the toothpick from his mouth. "No, but I assure you whatever is taking so long is not necessary. Although it's the first impression, believe me they are already impressed with you."

She beamed. "Let me find out you've been laying some flooring on my behalf. Sounds like something I ought to thank you for, later."

Walking to the car, Nile ogled her with pride. "Told you I'd always have your back. I tell you no lies. But you keep insinuating there's a reward for all my good behavior and we'll have to postpone this little meet and greet and hit them sheets."

"Agreed. I'm getting myself worked up too." Folding in her lips she motioned to zipper them shut.

They rode in silence. With Nile working the previous night's shift, exhaustion wasn't far off. If it weren't for his father's reminder of how much this brunch meant to his mother, he would've asked it to be moved to an early dinner. But then he'd be impeding on Joi's family traditions as well, and that was something he wasn't willing to do. *All the women in my life mad at me? Nah, that won't ever be a risk worth taking.*

He held her hand while he rang the doorbell. It was more of an announcement of their entrance, since the main door was already opened. The storm door was all that stood between them and their welcome. A friendly voice called out, "Coming, but come on in. If you don't belong in here though, my son's a cop and we do shoot."

Cinnamon wafted through Joi's nostrils, threatening to gurgle her tummy. She knew she'd regret not eating the night before, but her appetite wouldn't let it happen. Now she was standing at these people's front door hungrier than a starved mountain lion with a stomach full of gas.

Seemingly floating toward the couple was a woman whose skin was like a perfectly brewed cup of cappuccino. She met them in the foyer and helped Joi with her coat. Her makeup was light, and her smile was warm. Over her shoulder she updated her husband, "Grady, they're here. Get the camera ready. She's got it going on."

Joi blushed. The woman's old school compliment brought to mind her mother's insistence on doing the Electric Slide, every time she thought she was winning at something. Nile squeezed her hand. The glint in his eyes told of his zeal. How could she not be squeamish? At this point Joi wanted all to go well for his sake more than hers, which made her palms excrete, in turn causing her to attempt to pull her ligament away from his, despite his refusal.

After being kissed on both of her cheeks, Joi was being enveloped into Mrs. Ledger's modest bosom. *He must've told her how much I love warm hugs. Dang, what else did my dude tell her?* Nile's father joined as they guided the two into the dining room where the intricate holiday spread was on display. Accented with gold trim, the table runner fabric was a gray ombre with an array of multi-colored leaves running down its pattern. The placemats were the same, lined with sable cloth napkins rolled and held together by brass rings. The assortment of food rivaled that of a restaurant menu. In what Stephanie Ledger referred to as the *bread section*, there was a wooden bowl filled with buttered rolls, next to another wooden dish with cinnamon bites, beside four by four stacks of waffles. Meats were an assortment of ham, turkey bacon, sausage links, and steak with onions. A fresh fruit assortment was added to the mix by Mr. Ledger. To top it all off, while they stood behind their chairs, Mrs. Ledger returned from her disappearance into the kitchen with a bowl of scrambled eggs and a spinach quiche.

Joi tugged on Nile's sleeve and whispered in his ear, "I think I want to marry your Mom."

Overhearing, his father chuckled. "She is nothing short of amazing."

Camilla would say he's definitely meant to be my kin with them bat ears. Muffling her laugh, Joi tried to focus on the food.

"Oh honey, look at you, getting all embarrassed. I heard it too and I'm flattered. We want you to feel at home and since my darling, Nile, here, forgot to get back to me with your likes and dislikes, I thought it wise to cover all the bases. Once Grady says grace, serve yourself whatever you'd like."

Mr. Ledger took his wife's mention as the go ahead to ask everyone to bow their heads. "Lord, God, we thank you for this meal to nourish our bodies. Our son is healthy and strong, respected in the community he serves, and has finally found the woman who adds beats to his heart. We receive the blessing of having her in our home and pray that she too remains in good health and love. Place your hand over their togetherness, our union, our family near and far, immediate and extended. In the savior's name we pray, Amen."

As they all agreed in reverence and sat, Nile turned his phone on, checking for any missed emergencies. Holding his breath, he hoped he'd get to enjoy the meal without interruption. One behind the other, a flurry of text messages came across his screen, all reading with Liana's number as the sender. Out of respect for Joi he had removed the digits from his contacts. But there was no mistaking the sequence of sixes and nines. Choosing not to read whatever tidings his forgotten bedmate was trying to communicate; he placed the phone back in his pocket.

"Everything alright?" Reading his furrowed brow as a look of concern, Joi had made herself ready for Nile to inevitably excuse himself.

Taking her hand from his thigh and raising it to her lips, he assured her everything was fine. She shifted in her seat. *Why does that not feel like the truth?* She squinted her eyes, then nodded. Despite her apprehension, she allowed him to be satisfied with her agreement. Her plastered smile and soft voice pleasantries when his mother asked questions about her career path at the college would caution him. If he was smart, he'd devise a way to settle her discomfort.

"Joi, dear, when you're ready to start that business, please let me know. I think I'd like to get involved, as a possible investor but most definitely a volunteer. It's a noble cause and if done correctly, a business worth passing down to your children. Think of all the people you could help. There's so many who don't believe college is an option because they're afraid of the loans, but if you could help them find the money, you could realistically shift the education level of the local demographic."

Stephanie's sprightly offer softened Joi's demeanor. To be able to share her plans with yet another interested party was freeing.

Terrence and Camilla had long ago offered their assistance, but she believed it was because they would love her and want to help her with anything she did. But Nile found her dream endeavor attractive. And now his mother was here offering to put a foot in.

With each exchange between the women, Nile and his father traded glances. Grady Ledger gave his two cents from time to time, but it was clear Stephanie was on the road to adopting Joi and she would be getting most of her attention for the time she and Nile were visiting. By the time they had finished eating, not only had Joi's nerves settled, but she was beginning to feel as though she fit right in.

Helping to clear the table, Joi found herself alone with the woman of the house. She wondered if the aura would change or confirm her welcome. Particularly when the elder shooed the men away to the den. She paused just as Joi did when on his way out of the dining room, Nile's phone vibrated once again. Studying his shoulder slump, she tapped the metal tray of crumbs she carried in her hands. Joi observed him. It wasn't until he looked up and smiled, that she allowed herself to return to the clearing of the table.

As the women stood side by side at the kitchen sink, Mrs. Ledger rinsed the dishes while Joi loaded them in the dishwasher. Continuing to serve her kissable kindness, Stephanie expressed her final evaluation. "Joi, I anticipated loving you and couldn't be happier with who you are. Your hopes and aspirations are so aligned with Nile's, and together you guys can really be a beautiful force. I'm sure I'm embarrassing him, but I know my son. If you're here with us today, he believes you're someone special and I'm just glad he gave us old folks the chance to see why. We hope you'll join us again for something less formal sometime in the near future. Perhaps you and I can take a day of shopping. I can use an eye like yours to spruce up my wardrobe," she said eyeing Joi's pumps.

Almost missing the invitation, Joi was slow to respond as she looked off into the empty doorway. "Oh yes, yes. I'm sorry. Sometimes I get zapped into my head for a second. Shopping sounds perfect. Although, based upon your loungewear, I'd have to say there isn't a thing wrong with your eye." She swirled her pointed finger around in a circle.

The pair giggled like old friends. However, despite how hard she tried to remain out of her questioning thoughts, Joi couldn't get settled. *What are you keeping hidden, my love? And is it to keep us all safe or is it just you you're protecting?*

APPLE *pie*

Evening had given way to night. Beneath the porch lamp of the Briar household, Nile paced the outer doorstep. *It doesn't make sense to keep this from her. Making it into a bigger deal than what it is, isn't her style. At least I don't think so. But I already waited. She knows something's up.*

Once he had dropped Joi at her apartment to get ready for her evening with her own folks, he read through the previously ignored text messages. At first Liana seemed to be innocently wishing him a merry holiday. But then as he scrolled, pieces of what could be deemed as an apology came rolling in. Pictures of her in scantily clad lingerie came in like a photoshoot spread. She longed to be by his side as she was sure he had missed her also. While he sat in the front seat of his vehicle, still in the apartment parking lot, he wiped his palm down the length of his face. Not only had he not thought much about her, but he was thanking God he ended it when he did. Meeting Joi was the box of gifts that repetitively led to another.

Now as he sifted through the reasons for his anxiousness, he hoped Joi wasn't the jealous, rage throwing, lunatic Officer Gregory had pegged her to be. *This is silly. Why would I give what he said a second thought? This is my Joi we're talking about here. She knows my heart and it doesn't belong anywhere but in her hands.*

Just as he was about to press in the buttoned bell at the side of the entrance, the heavy oak door was pulled open. A face that appeared to be Joi's with thirty years added to it, peeked from behind it. Smiling as though an assumption had been confirmed, the woman stepped from the shadows and stood before him.

"As good-looking as you are, there's only one person you can be. I see now why my daughter is head over heels."

Nile grinned. He offered his hand. "Hello, Mrs. Briar. Nile Ledger." Once she accepted, he allowed himself to be pulled in for a hug. "It's a pleasure to meet you."

"Son, the pleasure is all mine, I assure you." But then she released him. Placing her hand at the center of his chest, she informed him, "You cannot come in just yet. I've been watching you wear away my Welcome mat for the past eight minutes. Now you can lie to me and tell me it was nervousness about meeting us, or you can tell me what the real deal is. But you're not going in there with any Christmas news to hurt my child."

Does every woman over fifty have the innate ability to read everyone's thoughts? What the hell am I supposed to tell her? That I've been trying to figure out how to tell her daughter that my ex has been sending me near naked pics? Sheesh! When I put it into words it sounds like a teenage boy problem.

"My ex has been texting me." The words spilled from his mouth.

Marjorie Briar folded her arms across her chest. Tapping her foot against the foyer tile, she waited. When there was no response from Nile, she probed. "And?"

Still trying to figure out why he felt not only obligated, but comfortable enough to tell his mind to a woman he literally just met, he was reminded to come back to the present moment. "Oh, I'm sorry. Yeah that would be weird if I left it at that. I don't want Liana or anything like that. It's been over for months. Way before I met Joi.

All day I've been gently letting her down, gently. Didn't want to be disrespectful, but you know, respecting Joi is always my top priority."

"Uh huh." She relaxed her arms. Chewing on her cheek, she was withholding a smirk.

"It's just, Joi had been seeing me ignore these advances all morning. I told her everything was okay, but I feel a way about not telling her who the messages were coming from. From what I've gotten to know about Joi, she trusts me, and I'd like to keep it that way." He studied the pavement like a child apologizing for breaking a window.

Slinking across Marjorie's lips was a smile bigger than a line of lakes. Her arms opened wide, she pulled him in for another embrace. "Come on in here, boy. Don't make no damn sense how a little love make you young people so scared of each other." Taking him by the hand she walked him in. She took his coat from him and hung it in the hall closet. "Joi is the more easy-going of my two, but both of my girls get their heads clear eventually. Tell her and it'll be nothing of a stink. It's really minor, silly even."

"What's minor?" a man's voice boomed.

Coming through the opposite entryway and making his way through the kitchen was none other than whom Nile recognized as, Terrence "Clique" Hamilton. Nile straightened his back. He and Joi had never discussed her relation to a notorious street runner of this caliber. Terrence once ran with the Grip Squad; a crime syndicate out in Wilmington. The crew was tied to drug trafficking, money laundering, illegal club operations, and although there could never be enough evidence gathered, murder. There had been a plethora of rumors as to why only a handful of the members could be brought to justice. One being they had an enforcer who moved through the darkened haze of the streets and alleyways, did the work of a few with his bare two, and left little residue. That same enforcer was also calculated. When he made a move, it was begrudgingly, so he negotiated, brokered truces, and was revered in more circles than the team's supposed man in charge.

Without experiencing any of the stories first-hand, Nile chucked it all up to speculation. He gathered it was the unit's urban legend, used to give them something to search the streets for. Until Clique had been arrested and there was his picture, the size of a loose-leaf, tacked to the cafeteria wall.

Still considered a newbie, three years in on the force Nile was thinking Terrence's tag was, Click believing it had something to do with the click of a gun. But bodies showing up with disfigured limbs and barely recognizable faces, the real was uncovered. Clique was showing up to scenes with a party of weapons, damaging crews as a one-man squad. Several years ago, after his arrest, the man faced trial. It seemed he'd pay for his accused crimes with his own life. But there was something, an error somewhere, no one could pinpoint who was to blame. It became a technicality. And just like that he was free. Shortly after, his name stopped ringing throughout the precincts. Most in the department assumed he relocated or met the demise on the streets they believed he was destined for.

Yet here he was, reaching to shake Nile's hand. "My wife, Camilla, has told me what she can about you. Nice to finally put a face to a name. You're a cop, so I'm guessing you know I'm Terrence."

They shook. Grips were firm. Two men determining their business.

Cutting through the ice, Camilla entered the kitchen, boisterous and with Kitty in tow. "Ain't nobody tell me the fam was here!" She hugged Nile then called for Joi to join them.

Kitty took a tour around Nile. At each point she took in another piece of him. Starting with his feet, then eventually looking up, squishing her brow, attempting to read his eyes. "Hmph. Seems alright to me." She paused and stuck her hand out to greet his. "I'm Auntie Joi's favorite person, Katoi. Even our names are similar. So, don't you go thinking you'll keep her away from us, taking up all her time and what not. We clear?"

Nile shook in agreement. "Wouldn't have it any other way. I promise you won't get any trouble out of me."

As soon as Joi set eyes on Nile, she sparkled all over. Containment was almost impossible as she glided over to his side. He leaned in to kiss her cheek, careful to not offend anyone. However, her skin warmed as though he had given her tongue and whispered the naughty things he'd like to do to her.

"Honey, if you keep grinning like a damn Cheshire cat, we'll soon have to fetch you some pain killers," Marjorie Briar joked, inciting the laughter of everyone in the room. With a plastic fork, she nonchalantly lifted a strawberry from the top of a piece of homemade, Fudge Turtle Crunch Cake.

"What's all the commotion?" Dressed in a plum velour sweat suit, Bruce came to join the party. Seeing Joi's arm wrapped around the waist of a young man he recognized from the department, he grinned and shoved his hand into his. "Hello, son. Bruce Magnus. I hear you're the reason our Joi is back to herself again."

"Oh Sir, I can't take credit for that. But I will let you keep me accountable for keeping that smile on her face."

"Yes, honey." Camilla snapped her fingers. She glanced at Terrence. Finally, there was a man that may be worth all of Joi's love. If Terrence gave her the nod, it would mean that he agreed.

Terrence held his palm up. He had to put a pause on Camilla's enthusiasm. There hadn't been time to vet the officer. However, with everyone's giddiness, he'd make it his duty to do so immediately.

Marjorie cleared her throat. "We've already done the gift exchange, but Nile, if you want something to eat, Joi can fix you a plate."

Terrence interjected. "You know what? Why don't you guys relax and let a couple of us men make our own plates for once? I know I could use a second helping."

Kitty giggled. "More like a third, Daddy."

"Yeah, yeah." He guided her out along with the rest of the crowd. "I'll be sure to bring you a slice of Nani's dessert cake. Bet you ain't complaining about anybody being on a third of that."

Joi looked back at Bruce. He answered her glare with a nod. She then double backed to Terrence. Before she could ask him to be nice, he mouthed, "I got you."

The last to head out, Bruce patted Nile's shoulder on his way.

Nile's phone vibrated. He ignored it. Liana had still been texting for reconciliation despite his admittance to dating someone new. He rubbed his neck.

"You need to get that?" Terrence pointed at Nile's hip.

"Nah, I'm good." Nile kept his cool. Accepting he was on Briar territory, he understood that meant it was his. There wasn't a question of Terrence's welcome in this house. Nile took note of the ease of his interactions. He was theirs and they were his.

"I left that life alone, you know," Terrence started. "This here, is my life now, my business."

Nile nodded. "I'm not in a position to doubt you. Your name hasn't been heard on my end in quite some time. Honestly, we all thought you moved away. A few considered you might've passed on but then we figured we would've at least heard that."

Stroking his chin, Terrence contemplated where the conversation might take them. "Understandable. But I wouldn't have run. Not without Camilla."

"Wow! I wouldn't have expected someone like you to admit being attached to a woman. Definitely not so freely. She must be some kind of special."

His cheeks reddened as he dipped his head. "Camilla is the Universe to me. This whole family is. They're all I've ever had. From the block to getting locked up, to helping me get free, they were all I ever needed. I'd do just about anything for any of them. Joi included." His tone became reflective.

Nile took a seat beside him at the island. *I guess everybody and everything ain't always what it seems.* "When I first met Joi, it was like I walked into the pages of a child's storybook or an afterlife, or something. Man, I don't know. Instantly, I wanted to love her, protect her, and ease all of her burdens."

"Same. When I met Cam, back in High School, her swagger had me. She'd walk around like everyone and everything was her footstool. Not in a way that made her mean or anything like that. Just confident. Her hair was always in this wild curly puff at the top of her head. She didn't fuss over makeup or who had eyes for her. She didn't roll with a gang of girls, never joined any of the teams, but everyone knew her name. The crazy thing was, no one was really privy to the real her, except that she was beastly protective over her little sister. Needless to say, she drew in my curiosity. That and the fact that she never held her tongue. Whatever she felt, she said it. Didn't matter if it was the person next to her or the teacher at the front of the classroom. At the time I thought she was a Goddess sent from another world," he chuckled. His eyes softened. The memories seemed to be renewing his appreciation for his now wife.

"I mean how does everyone know you and still not know you at the same time? For real, it was her who taught me how to move."

"So, she knew about your dealings? Because when I think of your reputation, I can't imagine you likening that to her protection."

"Everything isn't so black and white. At least it wasn't back then. She knew I hustled. Knew I had disagreements and settlements so to speak. But she never pried. Not like other girls. Camilla wanted to know as little as possible. She said she'd never be able to run her mouth if she had nothing to say. As much as I was trying to figure how to keep her protected from my enemies, she was doing what she could to keep me safe as well. It's always been that and probably will always be. Loyal couldn't even begin to describe this clan."

"And Bruce, how does he feel? I mean he has to know who you are, the things you're accused of doing. Being so prominent on the force at the time, the rumors had to come as a conflict of interests."

Terrence let out a hearty laugh. "Yo, my man, I do appreciate your attempt to not assume I was responsible for all the streets said I was." He nodded his respect. "Bruce is the one who got my hands clean for real. Taught me how to invest in some legal flips. Opened my eyes to the fact that I had a chance to live life right. Camilla deserved to have me try. And you do know Bruce isn't really their Uncle, right?"

It was Nile's turn to laugh. "Yeah. Joi explained to me that they started calling him that when he and Marjorie first started dating and they can't seem to let the title go."

"Don't get it twisted, though. He loves Joi and Camilla like his own seeds. Anything that disrupts their happiness, and he might as well be the doer of all *my* past deeds, you get me?"

Nile nodded. Clique was as serious as any man would be about his family. He admired how the ex-criminal approached things straight on. At the same time, it was also obvious he found his place of love and would do anything to keep it afloat.

Just then, Joi hopped back into the kitchen. "You guys don't look to be eating." She placed her hand over Nile's. "We good?"

He kissed her forehead. "I am. But I think we all know it's Terrence you really want to ask." He used his pointer to tilt her chin.

Terrence put his arm around his sister-in-law. "We're good. There's real in his eyes when he looks at you. He knows what it is, and I don't get no funny feelings of shade."

Joi blushed. "Glad to hear. Now let me hurry up and fix your plates. Camilla is on her way in here with intentions of eating from yours. She's going to be mad as hell if she finds she has to make one herself."

Declining Nile's offer to help, she busied with the already carved turkey, candied yams, collard greens, pineapple ham, and macaroni and cheese. Humming her good mood into the air, Nile's tap to the small of her back caught her off guard, causing her to flinch. "Geez, you scared me."

"My fault. But I have something to show you. I'm going to come clean in front of your known protector here, so you know my motives are always pure when it comes to you."

Terrence paused the gathering of their silverware. He had just given Nile the okay. He'd hate to have to renege already.

"Liana, my ex, has been the one making my phone vibe all day." He produced his phone and opened the screen to the text messages.

Butcher knife in hand, Joi released the section of ham she intended to slice and cleared her throat. "Okay." She skimmed the pleads for a meeting.

"As you can see, I've rejected her just as I will continue to do. But I could tell earlier when I said everything was alright, you felt differently. You questioned my character. We can't have that. You mean too much to me. I've never felt for anyone what I feel for you. Every time I look into your eyes, I see my future."

"Damn, man. You got me beat. All this from just a moment of unrest this morning? Apology before the end of the day? Don't let Camilla hear. I don't need any additional pressure," Terrence teased as he reached over Joi for a scoop of stuffing.

Cutting her eyes at him, Joi then returned her attention to Nile. "In the future, don't waste your time withholding this kind of thing from me. When Gordon approached me, I told you and you and I hadn't even been on a date yet."

"Wait, Gordon?" Terrence clanked his fork against his plate.

"Not now, T. Nile took care of it. And that's just it. I trust you, Nile, to take care of anything gunning for our happiness. As connected as we are, from the moment this thing between us started, I of course would feel any shifts in your energy. I appreciate you letting me know and I forgive you for being so foolish as to not tell me earlier. Just don't let it happen again."

Kissing his lips, she felt him tapping at her bottom. She could taste the appreciation on his mouth. If only he knew, there was solace now resting on her heart.

Breaking their lip lock, Joi made sure to mention, "Oh and please let ole girl know, I ain't no fighter, but my sister is. She's got to chill." She winked.

"Yes ma'am. Understood." He slid his tongue over his teeth. His reaction paused by Camilla's presence.

Terrence breathed a sigh of relief when the microwave dinged, indicating his plate had warmed. He kept his head down as his wife dipped a fork into his greens. She chewed as she eyed Nile. "You're still here and Terrence is cool with it. I guess that means we're family now."

SOUR CREAM *pound*

As early as seven, the morning of New Year's Day tempered the city. Every year the overnight hours came with reports of motor vehicle accidents, robberies, turf wars, and domestic disputes among the countless other complaints the operators received. If you were a police officer with the night off, you held your breath until the inevitable call to return to duty.

Nile was one of the lucky ones. He had no idea how he scored the night off on the Eve. Opting for dinner at Joi's with dimmed lights, a top one hundred music countdown, three bottles of wine, and the giftbox assortment from Sweet Thangs was a decision he appreciated throughout the night.

What started as a kickback, soon morphed into a sensual chocolate and berry feast where they fed on each other's hunger, drank from each other's fountains, filled each other up, spilled all that was within them, then whispered their way to replenishment. Lavender and Vanilla scented candles helped to create the shadows of lust against the walls. He and Joi's bodies intertwined, flexed, reached, bent, spread, and elevated for hours on end. Her scent of banana infused body butter was still running through his nostrils.

Still with the taste of her essence present in his memory, Nile breathed easy as he navigated his squad car on this New Year's Day. It didn't even bother him that Officer Gregory was asleep in the passenger. He rode past crews that hadn't turned in from the previous night, nodding his acknowledgements. Showing returned respect, they kept their hands in sight and grimaces to a minimum. Liquor stores had finally gated down and diners nourished the leftover partygoers. Sweet Thangs wouldn't open until nine, so for now he'd have to settle for a cup of the station's generic coffee. Riding around with half the beverage untouched, his good mood refused to be disturbed.

"All units. Calling all units. Disturbance on the five hundred blocks of Tattnall. Calling all units. Grade D. Ten, ten, fight in progress!" Sheryl's voice blared through the speakers.

Reaching over to the armrest, Nile activated the siren. He then tapped Daniel, who hadn't budged despite the staticky call for urgency. It took a second nudge before he was able to shake himself awake.

Backhand wiping the drool from his lips, Daniel Gregory sat straight up. He squinted at the intrusion of the sun through the window. "It's not even eight yet. Why didn't these fools kill each other last night instead? Now it's daylight. Stupid sons of bi..."

Nile stopped him. "Don't finish that thought. We're not disrespecting any mothers for the sins of their sons."

Daniel rolled his eyes. "Oh, I forgot. These are 'your people.' It's too bad they don't see it that way. You have to stop defending them at every turn. They're making the good ones with the good sense like you look bad."

Nile tried to keep focus on the road. He wrestled with the freedom of his tongue. *I swear if being racist was an actual crime, I'd baton him to death, and yet still put a round of bullets in him. Maybe straighten out that little dweebish hook nose of his.* Had he given his partner the attention he was begging for, they would be the reason the next emergency call came over squad car radios.

Nile smoothed the top of his head. Approaching their destination, he could see the thickening crowd. Several bystanders heard the sirens and dispersed while others turned their video phones toward him, egging the uniformed team on for reaction. Officer Gregory stood, watching the crowd while Nile got the attention of a passerby to shed light on what they'd be walking into.

Three other squad cars arrived seconds later. More of the crowd took leave. Each officer emerged with their vests. Nile sensed there would be fuel to the fire before an opportunity to understand what was going on. He stormed through the crowd, feverishly looking to get a handle on the unknown.

Two men, one looked to be about twenty-five while the other who bore resemblance to him could've been anywhere from forty to sixty. It was hard for Nile to tell with the man's missing front teeth, scruffy, balding hair, and ripped clothing. The older of the bickering pair pointed a jagged piece of timber at the younger.

"You're going to learn to respect me, today." He squared up, the branch as his bat.

Nile recognized the younger man as Terron, one of the gang members over on West Side. His rap sheet was extensive, but he had never served any real time. Just a few holiday weekends in county for disorderly conduct, resisting arrest, and a few marijuana charges. He never held onto large amounts though. And with the knowledge that the state decriminalized offenders for small amounts of possession, he never would. Despite his reputation for being a distributer.

Why is he out in Grade D? He shouldn't have any business here. According to Terron's file, he hadn't lived in the neighborhood for the past three years. With no solid address, he was the epitome of calling the streets his home. His mother moved out of state with her boyfriend the year before last and left her youngest daughter behind to fend for herself. His sister got her act together and went away to college in the Fall.

"Go ahead old man. If you swing, you better catch my dome and finish me." He stuck his neck out.

"Suit yourself,"

The man was mid swing when Nile stepped in and grabbed his weapon. "Let's not start the year like this. What's the problem here?"

"This little fucker called me a crackhead," the toothless complaint came with a slight wobble.

"Ain't you, though?" Terron smirked. He was enjoying being the agitator. It was a role he was named for playing in past cases. Not one that assigned him any real consequences just yet. However, if he didn't retreat, the old man was going to change that on the first day of the new year.

"Back up, Terron," Nile commanded.

"Nah, he 'bout that life. And when he do swing for real, I want him arrested for attempted assault. Y'all can't be picky with who y'all protect, right? I'm pressing charges," he said, baiting the aggressor with his smile.

A voice from the crowd threw out, "He's so disrespectful."

Another added, "Talking to his father like that. He treats him so bad and be the one selling him the drugs."

Nile looked between the two men. "You mean to tell me, the two of you are family and out here putting on this whole show for everyone to see? Come on, man. You got to do better than that." He put the ownness on Terron, seeing as though the accusation of being crack addicted might have had some truth to it. The community was riddled with substance abuse and guys like Terron only came around to make a dollar off the epidemic.

While the other officers assessed the situation to be less serious than anticipated, Officer Gregory finally decided to make his way through the dissipating circle of watchers. Barging through with a twelve-gauge shotgun pointed in the air, he swatted at phones and barked warnings, "Leave at once or you will all be arrested." His voice garnered the attention of Terron's crew who had been observing from across the street.

"Officer Gregory, I don't believe there's a need for that," Nile motioned toward the shotgun. "These two men are related, and I think we can settle this amicably. Isn't that right, Terron?"

Catching a glimpse of the group of young men, pulling up their jeans and tucking their hands in their waistbands, whatever bystanders remained, quickly filed out. They knew what the ten-man group was capable of. And they never missed a moment to make a name for themselves amongst the police.

From his peripheral, Nile also took note of the gang on its way. "Shit," he huffed beneath his breath. "Terron, back your crew down."

Suddenly the toothless father was his son's advocate. "Nah, Ron, don't listen to him. He's rolling with this white man who don't care about you or me. Coming over here with his big ole shot gun. Ain't nobody pulled a gun, but he got his out. We ain't going out like that." He folded his bottom lip over his gums and poked his chest out. Balled fists, his eyes bulged as he aimed to put fear into the toting officers heart.

"Officer Ledger, it would seem to me that it's your boy that you need to back down. He's the one with all the fire power."

Disregarding his ability to help regain control over the situation, Officer Gregory scoffed, "If I were you, I'd take my hand from my pants and hope that I don't believe you're holding anything but that soft ass dick of yours."

"What did you say to me?" Terron whipped his hand from his pants. What came with it was the grip on a Glock 19. He pointed it at Daniel Gregory.

ON alert, the other meandering officers had now drawn their weapons. They took up position behind their vehicles. It appeared the odds were not in Terron's favor.

Gregory bounced the shotgun into its click. Cocked and loaded, his sinister grin told of his hope that this opportunity would come. "Well, it looks like we're about to have a party." With speed, he took position and pointed the cannon, making Terron a clear target.

Nile held a palm up in either direction. "This has gone too far. Terron, put the gun down. Think of your sister. What do you think will happen to her when she hears you've died on these streets today? Don't throw your life away over a moment of hurt pride."

Terron cocked his gun. "Who says I'll be the one dying?"

"Look around you. There's six other officers with their guns drawn and they're all pointed at you. I don't know about you, but they've got enough to reload and load again. Unless you've played a sport that hasn't shown up in our files, you can't outrun that many bullets. And I for one, would rather not see you stretched on the pavement today."

"As a black man, I must say I do appreciate you Officer, but your buddy here thinks he can point a gun at me and hide behind its size. You want me to look around at y'all guns, but have you had a look around for real? My team strong. If I go down, I won't be the only one."

There was fire in his eyes. The old man he once argued with over name calling still held his protective stance. He'd go out in a hail if it meant telling, "the man," they weren't afraid of bullies.

Nile scanned the area, taking in his surroundings. Terron's army had doubled in size. There were twenty men all under the age of thirty each holding a firearm, and willing to put their lives at risk in the name of leveling the playing field.

"Drop your weapons," a neighboring officer yelled as he rested his arms over the hood of his police vehicle. He and his partner had pointed their attention to the increasing gang with various sizes of pistols. The car's radio could be heard with Sheryl putting out a call for backup.

"Put yours down," an unknown voice came from the array of guns.

Nile's heart beat a thousand times per second. Had he arrived at the location alone, he knew he would've been able to dissolve the situation without it coming to this. Officer Gregory winked at him, all too happy with his handywork.

Come on, Nile, think. I can't pull my gun out and threaten Gregory to put his down. Every cop on site would pin me as an enemy of the department. I'd probably die right alongside these young men here today. But I can't let this become a bloodbath. If someone would just step up with a cooler head, it doesn't have to be this. Just gotta find the one they will listen to. Nile caught the eye of who looked to be the senior of the gang. He bit his lip and motioned his head toward Terron. If he could get Terron to lower his Glock, then maybe the opposing fleet will see him as less of a threat.

The gang member looked to be shuffling his feet. He then moved out front. His gun was at his side, but then...

Pow!

Someone had let off the first shot. Each of the young brotherhood lacked hesitation when they sent their shots into the Officers' direction. The uniformed agents blasted in retaliation.

Nile was out of options. Drawing his gun, he scurried to take shelter. An overwhelming jolt to his rib, blew him forward. *If I hit this ground, I'm a dead man.* He found his way behind a dumpster. Reminding himself where he was hit, he was covered, he took deep breaths. *Dammit, Gregory, it didn't have to come to this.* After all the efforts put into building bonds for everything to be taken back to square one; it broke his heart. Yet, it was the pain that broke his flesh that stunned him. His pants leg was quickly becoming drenched with blood. His calve burned. People continued to scatter. He winced in pain, and yet had no knowledge of the culprit. His eyes found no one. His partners all took chase.

BLOOD *orange*

At nine thirty, the morning of New Year's Day, traffic had yet to pick up and Joi couldn't be more thankful. She spent the early hours after sunrise watching video of her niece, Kitty reciting an original poem at the church's Night Watch service. Her mother sent her pictures of the celebratory kiss she took with Bruce while watching fireworks on the riverfront. The turn of the year was proving to be one of true contentment and Joi could only feel grateful to God that this year she was sharing in the feeling.

After a long night of seduction, Joi realized why Nile was insistent on having his coffee every morning. Long days and body aches needed an inner soothing. As she pulled into the Sweet Thangs parking lot, she had made up her mind to let Anada make the Mintspresso with a tiny shot of expresso this time. *Maybe if she drowns it with milk and honey, I won't taste it.*

Locking her door, her heart skipped. A spark traveled up her spine. She surveyed the scene. Nothing was out of order. *Hmph. That's different.*

She thought back to the previous night's conversation. Nile asked if she'd ever consider living with a man again before marriage. *"Waking up to you every morning, knowing what's mine is yours, is a scenario I wouldn't mind having"* he said. Admittedly she was still apprehensive. Afraid of being that woman who would need convincing at every turn. Like he'd constantly need to prove to her, he was genuine and believed wholeheartedly she was made for him. But she took a deep breath then stared at herself in the storefront mirror. *Chill out. Don't have Nile out here trying to repair what Gordon couldn't keep whole. He is his own man. He'll inevitably make his own mistakes, as will I. But his heart has been speaking to mine since the moment we met. That's the conversation that matters.* She was reminded of the fires he had set to her body. The laughter they shared during random nights of shared cooking. His fingers and how they tiptoed up the small of her back when he was checking to see if she had fallen asleep. The look of interest when she chattered on about the makings of her day.

Entering the boutique café, Joi decided to order not only her drink, but Nile's preferred morning Prep. She'd text him to see where he was located so she could bring him his cup of friendly. That's what she had often heard him refer to it as. She laughed to herself. *He doesn't need no damn expresso to be kind. But I'll let him think that's what's necessary.*

"Good morning, my lovies." She greeted the three-woman team.

Anada, Anissa, and Vashti all responded with exuberant smiles.

"Ms. Anada, I need that mint tea you made last time and if you could squeeze in a pinch of expresso and then drown it in something, so I don't taste it, that would be great." Joi pinched her fingers together.

Anada laughed. "Let me make you a Mocha Mint Medley. We'll take it easy on the caffeine." She winked.

While Anissa scooted next to her boss and readied Nile's usual, Vashti added a lime frosted brownie to a powdered blue paper bag. She smiled at Joi, but the girl's nerves seemed rattled. Her normal upbeat personality was on mute. Pupils darting around the room, she appeared to be waiting for a guest that hadn't showed.

"V, you alright," Joi asked, concerned.

"Not really, Ms. Joi." She handed her Nile's packaged brownie and then began to retrieve a slice of cake for Joi.

That's when Joi noticed the shine on the young girl's face. Her eyes were glossy, and cheeks became flushed. Anada and Anissa had both paused to tend to her.

"Oh, my goodness, baby. What's wrong?" Anada wrapped her arms around Vashti, who had let a single tear fall.

"Something doesn't feel right. I was in my room this morning, lighting my candles and saying a prayer for all of us, you know so that we may continue to be blessed in the New Year. And a wind like a draft or something came in and blew all the flames out. None of the windows were open."

Anissa rubbed her back but spared no time in pushing Vashti to her point. "Did anything else happen, sis? It's not like you to be so torn up over such a thing. I mean I know you do your crystals and all, but..."

Vashti shook her head. "Everything just feels off and it's driving me mad that I can't put my finger on it. I feel sad even though everything has been perfect today. We opened, I was on time, and I didn't drop any trays. I even remembered to clean the steamer." She found it within herself to chuckle.

Ms. Anada brought over a hot cup of chamomile tea for Vashti to indulge.

Anissa hugged her friend. "I won't tell you not to worry because I know you read aura better than anyone I know. But I will tell you that whatever is wrong, we will all be by your side to help it get right."

At the sound of the windchimes, everyone looked to the front door. Gordon stepped in and to the counter. He hadn't noticed Joi, several feet away from him. "Large coffee, black. None of the extras."

Joi huffed and took a seat at a café table at the far end. She motioned for Vashti to join her. Anissa would handle Gordon's order.

Wiping her face with the back of her sleeve, Vashti took up her tea and accepted Joi's invitation. She was thankful for the care Joi had shown her. "I'm so glad you and Nile found each other. Even happier it was here." Her mood lightened.

Joi held her tongue. She knew if she spoke it would cause Gordon to react. *So, God, why are we doing this in the New Year exactly?*

Anada supplied the fresh brewed order while Anissa took payment. Neither of them aware, they were serving the man whose recklessness with Joi's heart had landed her in their shop as a committed customer. He was slow to leave, though. Scrolling through his phone as he baby-stepped toward the exit.

"Wow!" Gordon had paused his stepping. Holding the phone up in the air, he used his thumb to quickly swipe to additional screens. "That's crazy. Not even a whole day in and them jokers already having a shoot-out with the cops." He shook his head then proceeded out.

Joi's ears perked. Her next breath was lodged between her lungs and throat. Suddenly, the wool lining of her parka was uncomfortable, providing sweltering heat. All color had drained from her cheeks. Her lips trembling, her eyes met with Vashti's. There were no words either of them could conjure in their minds. The fear of what could be, plagued the air.

Anada rushed to find the remote for the mounted television. Finally snatching it from the counter behind her, she pressed for the power. The four women stared up at the screen. There was a gathering of reporters clamoring to ask questions of the Chief of Police and his gang of deputies stationed behind a podium. The background showed they were near the emergency entryway of a hospital. Across the bottom of the screen, the chyron read, "Police Officer Shot This Morning." A reporter narrated the scene, as Liana Bankman was helped to the front of a microphone. The made-up beauty with the golden, extensive ponytail, dabbed at her watering lids. Her plea for justice faded into the background as Joi heard the reporter referring to the woman as the girlfriend of Nile Ledger, the injured officer.

Overwhelmed by her thoughts, Joi's hands began to shake. *Nile?*

Shot? Oh my God, I've got to call his parents. She patted her pockets in search of her cellular phone.

"What the hell she mean, girlfriend? This damn chick." Anissa glowered as she worked to wipe a non-existent smudge with her rag.

Vashti jumped from her seat and raced around to Joi. Cloaking Joi with her arms, she passed on the love she had felt from Anada just moments ago. Feeling the young girl's drops of water that had already known it would need to fall, Joi's eyes had begun to sting as hers cascaded.

"Joi, you're shaking, baby." Anada came from around the counter.

Anissa followed behind, making a stop at the door to lock it and switch the sign to, "Closed." The emotions were heavy, particularly for the start of the year. However, she was glad she was able to keep listening to the press conference long enough to hear that Nile's gunshot wounds weren't life threatening and he was predicted to be out of the hospital in a matter of hours.

As Joi was being smothered by Vashti and Anada's layered embrace, her coat pocket vibrated. "Wait, I'm getting a call. Maybe it's Nile," she sniffled.

Her hands still trembling, she located the vibrating device in her inner pocket. She pulled it out and muttered her hello. The voice on the other end was shaken. "Joi?"

"Mrs. Ledger? I'm so sorry. I, uh, I was just about to call you. This is all so hard to believe." The tears were flowing freely. *How could I have not called her immediately? She must be going bonkers. And Mr. Ledger; he's probably ready to take out whoever did this. I can't blame him.*

"Joi, baby. Please stay calm. Grady is searching for parking. We're at the hospital now as we speak. I'm about to walk up to Nile's room. The nurse assured me, he's going to be okay, baby. Luckily, he was wearing a vest. The first bullet only bruised him a bit. That other one to his leg was painful, but they've already removed it. I just called because I didn't know if you were already up here or on your way."

"I just heard the news myself. Still in shock, honestly. But yes, I can meet you up there if that's okay." Thinking about the woman claiming to be Nile's girlfriend, Joi's heart sank. *Don't be selfish, Joi. The man was shot. It's better to know now than after you've lived with him for years.*

"I wouldn't want to intrude." Joi pulled her car keys from her strawberry red crossbody, then dropping them to the floor. Holding the phone to her ear, she tried reaching beneath the table. *This day just keeps getting better, doesn't it?*

Vashti was quick to bend below and retrieve the keys. Anissa stood by the door and unlocked it. Anada helped Joi up from the table.

"They said it's not serious, so we may not stay long. Just have to lay eyes on him. He's still my baby boy after all. We may not be there by the time you reach, but Joi?"

"Yes, Mrs. Ledger?" Joi hoped the woman wasn't about to apologize for her son's indiscretions. Even if she knew he was still involved with Liana, it was his place to leave Joi out of his web. *I just don't understand why he would jump through all those hoops to show me the text messages. Like why even take it there?*

"You're family, never out of place."

A shy smile was all Joi could bring herself to offer the world. What the woman said was endearing, but if it wasn't Nile's truth, no one could make it so. Not even a directive from his mama. *I just wish I didn't love him.*

"Listen, I saw that little heifer making a name for herself among the crowd. If I weren't so concerned with getting the word on my son, I would've shut that nonsense down myself. Don't worry about her. And if I don't see you when you get here, just know we love you and soon as Nile is out, you make sure to bring him across my threshold."

"Yes ma'am."

After giving the girls the rundown on Stephanie Ledger's phone call, Joi noticed Vashti drying her tears. They were all relieved to know Nile would not be leaving the earth anytime soon. Although, Joi was still nursing the wound in her heart.

As Joi headed out, Vashti grabbed the forgotten bag of brownie and shoved it in her hand. She kissed Joi's cheek and then passed the boxed cake Anissa had just finished ribboning. "Your brownie and his cake. Bite into one another's love and you'll see you're really one in the same. Don't let a lie that wasn't his change that."

CHEESE puff

Grady and Stephanie Ledger held hands as the left Nile's hospital room. Although this was the day, they had all been hoping would never come, they appreciated knowing he was alive and well. From around the hallway bend, Liana looked on until she was sure they had stepped onto the elevator. Once she heard the doors closing, she traipsed in to see Nile.

"Oh my, honey! Are you okay?" Liana rushed over to the laying officer.

She spread her arms open wide, dramatically collapsing atop of him. His neck still smelling of the cologne she had missed, she nestled in for a bit. Inhaling the aroma, she was reminded of what should have been.

Nile's body stiffened. Cautioning himself to not be offensive, he lightly tapped her back. When she still hadn't risen, he gently pushed. "Okay, that's enough."

Liana stood in disbelief of his candor. "Enough? Nile, you had a bullet in you. How can you be so calm? I knew this would happen. Of course, this isn't the right time to say, I told you so, but…" She made a fuss, attempting to prop an additional pillow beneath his foot.

"Liana give it a rest. I'm not dead and this is all part of my job.

Besides, it was more like a graze the way it tore my skin. Not the whole bullet, like you say, and it took them almost no time to remove the fragment. Because you were able to predict something that's commonplace in my line of work doesn't make you right." Using his strength to lift himself, he was now sitting straight up.

Adorned in a white, wool, trench coat, she folded her arms. Tapping her foot as though she was waiting for him to come to his senses, she huffed. "I'm not your enemy. It's asinine for you to berate me whenever I show some genuine care for you."

He studied the bandages wrapped around his calve before answering her. It truly wasn't her fault she felt how she did. There wasn't anyone to blame for them being on two different fields when it came to how they thought. Still, she was forcing herself back into his life and it was something he couldn't tolerate. Not with the way Joi was opening up to him. If his prayers continued to be answered, she would be the next Mrs. Ledger. Thinking back to when Joi admitted she didn't want to live without him, he was determined she'd know he felt the same. Liana would have to swallow the rejection.

"I need to get out of here."

"Excuse me?" Immediately, she relaxed her stance. Slowly, she returned to his bedside. Pouting, she relied on the brat like expression that had most men eating out the palm of her hand.

Swinging his legs over the side of the bed, he could feel the rush of blood. *Being laid up for hours in a bed that's not your own is only good if Joi's next to me.* He reached for his phone. She hadn't called nor sent a text. His mother told him about the press conference and her chat with Joi. He knew his baby. She wouldn't receive a promise of his love from anyone but him.

Liana snatched the phone from Nile and rested it back on the wooden replica of a nightstand, beside the bed. "Oh no, who you calling? Baby, you have to get well. I'm going to take good care of you." She tried leaning him back.

"What is happening?" Nile snickered at the ridiculousness of her actions.

She blinked three times, purposefully, before replying. "Nile, we can't go on like this." Her proper tone returned as opposed to the high pitch character disguise she had been putting on.

"This..." she snaked her hand down his leg, gingerly touching the wounded area. "This is why we parted. Do you get me? I was just looking out for you and being the hardheaded, got to have my cape, world rescuer you are, you punished me for it. Now look at you. You've been shot by some kids who don't even care enough to keep their own mothers safe."

"First of all, we don't know who shot me. And second of all, it was my own department members that agitated the situation. Furthering my point that our community needs people who will have their best interests in heart. Not those who write them all off as unsalvageable parts."

She held his hand. "And that's what makes you so great. All you see is the beauty in people. Even with physical damage, you're not ready to give up. So why may I ask, are you so willing to give me up?" She was speaking sweetly, rubbing her thumb over his knuckles.

He took back ownership of his limb and sighed. "It was only a week ago that I told you I was in love with someone else and still you act as though you forgot. Whatever the reason for our break-up, it matters none when my heart fully belongs to another woman."

Returning to herself, Liana scoffed. "Are you serious? Who could be better for you than me? And, where is she? 'Cause as far as I can see, I'm the only one here." She pretended to search the room.

Nile bit down on his lip. *If you weren't out there parading around like you're my woman, maybe she would be.* "Liana, I tried to be nice. Really, I have. But it seems you only respond to aggression, which is a shame because that ain't me. Still it appears to me that kid gloves don't work for you. So, here it is. You're not for me. Never was. That's why it took so long for me to take you out and for that matter take you down. Although you are beautiful, you're spoiled and pretty classless. It has always pained me to know you used visits to your grandmother to track me down. She probably thought you were getting over your detest for the neighborhood you grew up in and found it more of a priority to give her your time and attention. You're in my room, using my weak ass injury as a way to weasel your way back into a dead situation. I told you I have a woman. But I just don't have one. I have the only woman for me. Violating her is definitely not a way to get on my good side. And now since you've told the world she has something to worry about, I have to go fix it. But the thing about her is, she knows me. I mean really knows me. Your little stunt may have ruffled a few feathers but best believe the only wings you've you clipped are your own. So now if you please, see yourself out." He pointed at the door.

Mouth agape, Liana was at a loss for words. If she wasn't so sure the hospital security team would throw her over a shoulder and carry her out of there, embarrassing her to no end, she'd hurl the retro corded phone on his nightstand through the window. Instead, she snatched her oversized Gucci signature pocketbook from the armchair, turned herself around, and stomped out. If he wanted to be with a woman who was less than her, so be it.

BUTTER*cup*

"Mommy, I can't go in there. What if she's there with him? I can't stand by and watch another woman love on him. It would hurt too much."

White knuckle gripping her steering wheel, Joi's tearful plea to her mother had been going on for the past thirty minutes. She had been sitting in her car in the first row of the emergency parking area, awaiting the gall to step inside the hospital. It never came.

"Oh honey, don't let this woman ruin what the two of you have. I saw the way Nile looks at you. And you know, your brother-in-law gave his stamp of approval. Bruce did some digging. Nile is as stand up as they come. If this is that same girl with the text messages, honey I think she's just creating mountains where there is only sand. But you won't know until you talk to him. Just answer his call."

Even though she nodded her agreement, Joi still couldn't let herself be so bold. Facing her windshield, she stared out into the dreary day, wishing for a solidified sign that the feverous love she shared with Nile, wasn't just a lukewarm fling for him to pass the time. "Just when I thought I was making friends with the Universe again," she whimpered.

"Well baby, Camilla and Terrence ought to be there to keep you company soon. That's if they aren't there searching for you already. Sit tight. You know your sister won't let you sit in sorrow for too long."

Joi bolted up. "What? How'd they know where I was?" Snatching her bag from the passenger seat, she rummaged for tissue.

"Girl, you're crazy for real. You think you're the only one who watched that little makeshift press conference or whatever they want to call that mess? Soon as we received the alerts, Milla was on my line asking if I heard from you. Terrence was putting in calls to his connects asking if they knew who pulled the trigger. And once that little bittie showed her face like she was Nile's soon to be wife, Milla damn near jumped through the roof. I could hear Terrence in the background trying to talk her out of finding the girl to thump a shoe heel through her skull. She never did play when it came to you."

Without finding what she was searching for, Joi finger smudged her lids dry. "Mama, they can't come up here. I'm not even sure if I'm going in. And you know Camilla is going to act straight fool. Getting arrested at my age was so humiliating. I never want that to happen again over being jilted."

"Girl, that's your problem. You can't get over anything. That happened and it's in the past. But don't you worry. I told her not to go and have the people keep her in the asylum. She's coming because you need someone other than me to grow you up. Hiding in your car when the man you love is suffering from an occupational hazard will do no one any good. He needs you and you're all inside your feelings over something that don't even sound right. You don't listen to me, but I know you'll get your ass up for her, if for no other reason than to convince her not to exacerbate the situation."

A knock to her driver's window, pulled Joi from the studying of her cuticles. Camilla, earring free, and stone-faced, looked her square in the eyes. "You talking to Mama?"

"Yeah, but listen, I don't want..."

"Aht-aht." Camilla pulled the car door open. "Don't nobody know your pain like I do and we ain't fittin' ta have you revisit your depths of hell. Kitty is over the moon with you returning to yourself and she swears Nile is the second coming of Jesus." She tugged at Joi's elbow.

"Goodness, Ma, she's trying to drag me out the car." Joi reluctantly gave in to her sister's pull while keeping her mother on speaker phone.

"Joi, baby, do what she says minus anything that will have us posting bail. Face your fears pumpkin. If it's what you imagine, then it will hurt, but you will heal. But if it's what you know, then you'll be reminded to judge him based upon his own character and not the sum of your past." Marjorie Briar ended the call. Nothing else needed to be said. Joi would have to make it through this hurdle. Camilla would make sure of it.

Camilla put her palm to Joi's cheek. "Mama's right. How can you mend if you keep letting all that old shit rule you? I know you're scared to be out there, heart dangling for anyone to take a swipe at. But he caught it. Wrapped his fingers around it then squeezed life back into it. My dear sister, that kind of love doesn't break you. It nourishes you and drinks up every ounce of love you pour back into it. You know if I thought he was playing with you, I would've been let him have it," she teased.

Joi smirked. Releasing her pent-up breath, she admitted, "This I know."

"But hold that thought, cause there that trick go."

Time was not something Camilla was willing to spend on waiting for Joi's reply. She powerwalked toward a visibly flustered, Liana. As if she were accompanied by a large faction, Camilla stood before her, blocking her path.

"So, you like drama?"

Stunned there was this unfamiliar woman in front of her, Liana was annoyed. "Oh brother. Who are you supposed to be?"

Once Joi caught up with her sister, she realized what would eventually evolve would be nearly impossible to contain. She took a deep breath. "Come on, she's not worth it. I'll go up."

Camilla stepped closer. "Who do you think I am?" Holding her pointer and middle fingers like a gun, she pressed them against the side of Liana's head.

"Bitch don't touch me," Liana shrieked in disgust.

"Shit," Joi muttered beneath her breath. If there was one thing Camilla would not stand for, it was being called out of her name. *This is ridiculous. She can't fight all of my battles. And you know what, Nile has shown me nothing but love and respect. For whatever reason, this woman can't let him go, but I'm making that more of my issue than it needs to be. Mama is right.*

Just as Camilla drew her arm back, Joi caught it. She pulled her sister back and took her place. "Look, I don't know who you are other than the woman who was begging Nile to come back to her. Just like you aren't privy to who I am other than the person who is saving your life right now. We're all adults and I don't plan to be out here showing my ass like I'm filming for a reality series. However, let me tell you this: if I find out you purposely misrepresented yourself in order to finagle your way back into a slot that's already been filled, what seems to be a random approach in a hospital lot, will be the least of your worries. Am I understood?"

Reaching some clarity about who she was facing, Liana hurriedly nodded. She watched as the two women walked off, the less aggressive one, leading the other. Not a woman who would ever come to blows over a man, she had been made to accept she was out of the picture for good.

HARD cookies

NILE SAT IN HIS HOSPITAL ROOM ARMCHAIR. POSTED ATOP A pillow resting on an ottoman, his leg was stretched. While awaiting the nurse's return with his discharge papers, he scrolled through his social media accounts. No postings from Joi. He knew he should try calling her again, but he had yet to figure out what to say. *Liana did that all on her own. I had nothing to do with it. No, that's too accusatory. Listen baby, you're the only one for me. Okay that sounds like it came straight from the cheating man's handbook. Dammit! I didn't cheat. But why would she believe that? Everything's pointing in all kinds of directions.*

A knocking at the hospital room door, jarred him from his thoughts. "Come in."

In walked Terrence, his disapproving glower unmistakable. Giving Nile the onceover, he busied over to the window, splitting the blinds and observing the parking area. He huffed, then turned back to Nile.

"If you're here, I take it Joi isn't coming." Nile sighed. "Lay it on me." Accepting his fate, his eyes met with Terrence's. *Just please don't tell me I've caused her to run. She has to know I'm nothing like that weak ass ex of hers.*

Terrence swiped his palm over the length of his face. "Bruh! What you mean lay it on you? Do you understand that if things are as thick as they're looking, I'm going to have to lay you down? There's no other way. I just don't get it. You had my respect from the rip, nothing like that other goofball she used to date. I really thought you and I were about to be on some brother shit."

Nile shook his head. *He's definitely taking it too far with that old gangster shit. Someone already tried to take me out and we see ain't nothing but some torn flesh.* "Coming from you, I know that's an enormous compliment. And no, it's not what it looks like. Liana is my ex and despite whatever she portrayed, she and I haven't had anything going on since nearly a year ago. Joi is the only woman in my line of vision. Nothing and no one would ever compare to her. I love her, bro." Touched by his own sentiment, his voice was becoming strained.

Breathing a sigh of relief, Terrence nodded. "Okay. So, go get her then."

"Dude, you don't think I know I need to talk to her? She won't accept my calls. Text messages all went unanswered. The nurse out there taking her sweet time discharging me. My mother said Joi was on her way when she spoke to her last, but I know it wouldn't take her this long if she wasn't feeling some kind of way."

"Man, that girl been downstairs all this time. Debating if she's ready to get her heart broken again. Got Camilla ready to burn these blocks down. Crazy too, cause Milla is on your side. She knew from jump that broad was lying. Me, I said I'd come talk to you man to man to see what it is. Look you in the eye and shit."

Nile chuckled. "I swear y'all got to be the realest and the wildest combination of family members I've ever known."

"Don't act like we never said how it goes down," Terrence pointed out as he strolled back over to the window.

Taking note of the second visit, Nile furrowed his brow. "Did you bring an army you're waiting for? Should I grab my gun? You keep peering out of the window like you're waiting for a bomb to strike."

Terrence smirked as he looked back. "First of all, you already know about me. No army. Second, I'm hoping Camilla don't get Joi arrested again because I see that she caught up with your so-called ex. You know if she trip off her rocker, I got to go off too, on general purpose."

Nile gripped the arms of the armchair and rose. "Do me a favor and call the nurse. This is getting out of hand. There will never be reason enough for her to be out of character over me. I'd lose my own character before I let her put hers on the line."

Terrence stroked his chin as he watched Nile hobble over to the bed. "That's what I'm talking about, champ. If you bout to strap up to go get Joi, I'm with it. I'll take you to her right now. Even if she leave, I'll take you to Mama's house because you know that's where she's going."

Nile pulled the hooded sweatshirt his parents brought to him earlier, over his head. "I swear you don't quit. It's actually admirable when I think about it." He stood, grabbing his keys from the rolling tray.

Terrence reached for Nile's coat from the narrow closet beside the bathroom. He told himself to remain quiet. Nile would assert himself as the man he was believed to be. It was hard, having insight on Joi's past agony. He had seen her grow up and not once did she stray from the sincere sweetness, she had earned the reputation of being.

"Look, I appreciate you. There isn't a person in a world who would be able to predict my respect for you." He snatched his coat and doubled it under his arm.

"I too was starting to see you as family. And if I can help it, we'll continue to build. But if Joi is upset with me, then it's me who has to get it right with her. There isn't a place on this green earth she would be able to go, without me finding her and doing whatever I can to get us back to where we were. Am I going to go get her? Absolutely. But all I need from you is to hold that door open for me."

Terrence was impressed. No man under his wing had ever

rejected his help. But Nile wasn't under him. He was a man that would stand as tall as any man that had taken on loving the Briar women. Without a second more of hesitation, he darted to the wooden door and opened it. Only, there was no need to wait for Nile to limp through. He was face to face with Joi standing on the other side.

SWEETbread

Joi's looked up into her brother-in-law's eyes. Her heart pounded as she hoped not to have him break the news that Nile was not the man, she believed him to be. However, he remained mum. Instead, he stepped aside, allowing her entry into the single hospital room.

Camilla strode in behind her. She poised herself beside her husband. Together they watched Joi gallantly place herself directly in front of the man she had been afraid of not loving her. Staring into his face, Joi searched his eyes for the truth, everyone seemed to have concluded. Camilla slipped her hand in Terrence's. Watching her sister be blanketed in the arms of someone who without a doubt would hold her until whatever tidal wave of emotions had surrendered, glossed her eyes.

Nile let his coat fall to the ground. He kissed Joi's forehead. Her face in the center of his palms, he thumbed away her tears. Beholding her beauty, he looked into her soul hoping she saw that his was present.

Terrence tapped his wife's thigh. "Come on. Let's give them some privacy." He turned her around, gripping her waist as he followed her out.

"T, they just so beautiful. Makes me think of us when we were just falling for each other." She dabbed her falling tears.

He dipped his head in the crevice of her neck. "Speaking of memories, I saw an empty spot in the lot way off in the corner. Let me remind you of why you love me with your little gangster self. Don't think I didn't see you about to lose your sexy ass cool."

As her elder sister picked up the pace in her sway, Joi rolled her eyes. She looked back up at Nile. "They have no boundaries," she said, shaking her head.

Nile grinned. "I don't know. They're kind of cute." He continued being mesmerized by the effortless glow of her skin. *Still as beautiful as the first day I laid eyes on her.*

"You think so?" Remnants of her smile appeared across her face. Although, the uptake was slow, she was returning to him.

"Joi, whatever seed of distrust I allowed to be planted, I'm sorry. Today was tough. For the both of us. But please don't take me for anybody's fool. I can only get through times like this knowing it's you that I get to come home to. No one else."

She squeezed her arms around his waist. "Every single fear I've had about you and I seemed to come to life today. The heart palpitations that come with the dread of believing your life could be hanging in the balance. And then the intimidation that doubt brings. I guess all along I was afraid you, this, we were too good to be true."

Puffing through his nostrils, Nile pulled her into his torso. He stroked her hair. Feeling the sting of his fresh wound, he was forced to take a seat on the bed. But once he did, he kept hold of his Joi, her hands in his.

"By no means am I a perfect man. But Liana, or any other woman for that matter, is not the kind of mistake I would make. Every day I put my life at risk. Only a fool would do the same with his heart. It amazes me that you could think there would ever be another choice for me when I thank God, daily, you chose me."

Pressing her lips against his, she invaded his mouth with her tongue. His greedily took hers in, laying layer after layer of love. The taste of his words danced around her mouth. His firm grip to the small of her back sent currents through her spine. He was pulling her further in and she was compelled to let him. Stradling his lap, she trusted him to hold her.

Breaking their kiss, Nile smiled. "You smell like, Sweet Thangs."

"Oh yeah? The girls sent your brownie. I've got it in the car if you want me to run and go get it."

Unable to go another second without another taste of her lips, he lightly snatched her bottom lip between his teeth. "Nah, I rather you run and find that damn nurse to discharge me. I'm trying to get you home and see if *you* still taste like cake."

epilogue

November had come around once again. Winds were more aggressive than they had been in previous years. The sky seemed to hint a sprinkling of snow. Still the, Sunrise Sugar Rush was buzzing with its morning excitement.

"Good morning, Nile," Anada greeted with a knowing smile.

Every day she made sure to greet him. Although she had in the past, the first of the year scare reminded her of just how precious life was. The chaos that ensued with Officer Gregory being placed on leave due to his part in aggravating the incident to possible deadly levels, was one for the record books. It was weeks before the news channels finally stopped covering the story.

It had also had a profound impact on Anada's husband, Dylan. He would now drive her to the shop every morning, stick around for an hour or so before leaving to set out on his day. He also began stopping in during his afternoon breaks, finally catching Nile and extending an invite for he and Joi to join them for dinner.

Caramel and Vanilla begging the plain clothes officer to indulge, floated through the air. If he could just have a sip, Nile would be able to breathe easy. But no, the caffeine would add jitters to already unstable nerves.

"You ready?" Anissa smiled as she poured him a glass of filtered water. The lemon and orange wedges along with cucumber slices, was the most she could offer.

He took a swig. Taking in the light beverage, he did feel refreshed and was thankful for the remedy. There was an assortment of bite sixed treats line across the glass casing. His fingers itched to grab one just to stay busy.

"She'll be here. Don't worry." Vashti soothed with a grin as she carried a tray of punch cups filled with multi-colored rose petals.

The doorway's windchimes made their music. Nile turned his head to see Joi walking through. Toting her sincere smile, the one he loved to see grace her face, she walked straight to him.

"Good morning, Mr. Ledger. Coffee on your day off, huh? Someone must've put it on you last night." Her tone deeply seductive, it oozed of the night's entanglement. She tipped on her toes and kissed his lips.

Mint seeping from her breath, her hand placed squarely in the middle of his chest, she had him as intoxicated as the fateful day she excused herself to be let into the cafe. Although, now she never hung her head. Her features were bright under the maroon fedora which housed her shoulder length curls. Wrapped in a matching belted wool trench, she strutted to the counter, placing her order for cake.

Although Anada appeesed her request, she asked, "You think you still need this to thrive? Seems like you've found your own bottomless well of chocolate to get you through."

Joi blushed. She whispered, "He is everything, isn't he?"

Nodding in Nile's direction, Anada agreed. "Oh Joi, yes he is." A single tear ran down her cheek.

"Oh, my goodness, Ms. Anada, are you okay?"

Joi ransacked her pockets for tissue. She looked to call out to Anissa for assistance, but she now was nowhere to be seen. Twirling around in search of Vashti, she was taken aback by the scene. The patrons had all made a circle around her. Nile was at the center, on bended knee, holding a chocolate oval shaped diamond ring up in question.

Looking around again at the faces of these random customers she realized, they weren't there by chance. Her mother held hands with Bruce who stood beside Camilla. She clutched the fingers of Kitty who also held the hand of her father. Terrence's stance led to Stephanie Ledger's as she giggled beside her husband, Grady. Filling the other links, were her co-workers (minus the now graduate, Caprice), Sheryl, Vashti, and Anissa. Anada came from around the bend, and joined in.

"Babe, here. Focus." Nile's request prompted the laughter of the crowd.

Joi turned to him. Glossy eyed and rose cheeked, she fought back the fountain of tears pushing for freedom. Nodding her head, she was at a loss for words.

"Joi, you are in every sense of your name, my rib. My days are brighter, my heart is stronger, my purpose is clearer, all because I have you as my partner in life. If you say, yes, I will forever work to keep you saying yes over and over again. Joi Anita Briar, will you do me the honor of being my wife?"

The damn had broken. Tears flowed like rivers down her face. Joi placed her hand in Nile's, accepting the ring. Watching him glide it down her finger, she found the voice to mutter, "Yes." She repeated her reply but this time with a shout, "Yes!"

He rose to meet her lips. Applause was the melody they'd hear for minutes on end. Each in attendance tossing rose petals at the couple, she had been showered with flowers of all colors, but most importantly, she'd be forever showered in his love. And he would relish in hers.

AFTERWORD

Hello and thank you for taking this journey of sweet love with me. As this was my first full on romance novel, it was both thrilling and terrifying to write. However, I hope your heart leapt just as mine did when Nile and Joi planted their love in each other's lives. Spirit shifts when you're in the presence of your destiny has always been an intriguing thought to me. I'm a hopeful romantic who believes in love at first sight, first kiss, first touch, all of that.

Whatever your thoughts, please be so kind to share them in the form of a review/rating. If you stick with me, I promise there's more love to come.

Many Blessings!

SOCIAL MEDIA

READER GROUP: PHOENIX FIYAH FLIES IS NOW ON FACEBOOK!

Twitter: @pwrites
Instagram: @pwrites
Spotify: Life As P (podcast)
Apple Podcasts: Life As P
iHeart Radio Podcasts: Life As P

OTHER TITLES BY PHOENIX ASH

Cookies & Crumbles

Soiled Sheets

Made in the USA
Middletown, DE
19 January 2025